the unfinish‹

J S Matthew

With best wishes!

J. S. Matthew.

Ravenshead Publications

The author has taught for many years in various institutions of Higher Education. This satirical thriller is his first novel. He lives in Yorkshire with his wife, and has a grown up family.

PRINTED BY MORECAMBE PRESS 01524 66555

Chapter 1

The leafy campus of Parkdale College was quiet under the cloudy sky of an early spring morning. The chirping of the birds was the only sound to be heard. The curtains of the small but tidy office of Dr Delia Bumstead, lecturer in English language and literature in the Department of Social and Language Studies, occasionally stirred in the gentle breeze. But all was still.

Indeed, Dr Delia Bumstead was very still.

She was sitting at her desk, her hand gripping the mouse of her computer. In front of her, the screen waited for her to finish the email she had been about to send to the Head of Department and other assorted colleagues. But her email had been unexpectedly interrupted.

Savagely interrupted.

Dr Delia Bumstead's short dark hair was clotted with blood as her head lay on her desk, her lifeless eyes staring manically at the mug of coffee to her right, in which one of her contact lenses floated listlessly.

The silence was broken by footsteps down the corridor. Anne Dickinson, a second-year student of English and French, arrived at Delia's door and knocked. When she got no reply, she knocked again, a little more loudly. Thinking she heard a sound from within, she opened the door and went in.

Anne's screams could be heard from outside the building.

"God, this is awful! I can't believe it! Someone please tell me it's just an awful dream, and I'll wake up soon!"

Rosemary Hepworth was about to say more, when she let out a series of sobs and buried her mascara-stained face in yet another tissue as she sat behind her desk.

The departmental secretary allowed herself to be comforted against the ample chest of a middle-aged woman in dungarees, with short spiky grey hair and round tinted glasses.

"All right, Rosemary, darling, it's all right. I'm here."

The secretary slowly extricated herself and took a mirror from her handbag. She looked at it as she gently dabbed at her reddened eyes and rearranged her blond hair.

"Oh, thank you, Veronica." Her lip trembled, then she managed to control herself. "Who… who found her, did you say?"

Veronica Makepeace put an arm around her shoulder. "Anne Dickinson, dear. You know her, one of the second years. A nice girl, but a bit conventional. She's in my Social Policy group."

When Rosemary started to cry again, Veronica brought a chair across to her desk and gently stroked her head.

"And what's all this? Just what's going on?"

The speaker was another woman, tall and thin in an expensive looking two-piece suit, who had noiselessly pushed open the door bearing the notice *Office and Enquiries*.

"It's all right, Harriet-"

"Is it now? It doesn't look all right to me! And you always told me that I was the only one!"

"Harriet, listen-"

"No, *you* listen!" She pointed an angry finger. "I want to know how long this has been going on!"

"Harriet, don't be silly! Something awful has happened! There's nothing going on! I can explain everything!"

Harriet Bond glared at her from over her glasses. "I should hope you can – otherwise, tonight you're sleeping in the other room! I'll see you later – and it's your turn to cook, don't forget!"

Before Veronica could say another word, Harriet swept out of the office, muttering something about fidelity, almost knocking over a tall, fair-haired young woman in a blue and white striped blouse and black trousers who was just coming in.

Harriet Bond's accusations had upset Veronica Makepeace so much that, like Rosemary, she was crying.

"What is the matter? Why are you both upset?" The young woman's voice betrayed a slight German accent.

"Oh, Ingrid, it's Delia…"

"Oh, yes, and what's new?" She put her hands on her hips. "What has that woman managed to do this time? Who has she upset now?"

Veronica blew her nose before replying. "It isn't what she's done, Ingrid, it's what has been done to *her*!"

Ingrid's blue eyes narrowed. "What do you mean?"

"Oh God, she's been…"

The German tilted her head. "Yes, go on, Rosemary. She has been what?"

But the secretary was unable to say the words, so Veronica said them for her.

"She's been murdered, Ingrid."

"What?"

"Who's been murdered, then?"

The nasal Merseyside tones of Mick O'Reilly, a big burly man in his early fifties, and who was the Head of the English section, filled the room.

"Murdered?" Ingrid stared at Veronica.

Mick O'Reilly slowly ran his hand through his thick grey hair, his smile disappearing. "Er, who's been murdered?" He looked at each of them in turn. What's all this about?"

"Delia's been murdered, Mick."

"What?"

"Delia's been murdered. Here, in her office." Rosemary spoke quietly and almost dispassionately, somehow having regained her composure.

"In her office? This morning?" He slowly put down his briefcase, his eyes flitting from one person to another. "Is she... is she in there now?"

"Yes. One of the second years, Anne Dickinson, found her. The police are on their way."

"And how's Anne?"

"She's with nurse Richmond in the student medical centre."

"God, it's awful," said Veronica. "I just can't imagine who would do such a terrible thing."

Ingrid Kaltz slowly folded her arms and rested her backside against the office counter, her eyes seemingly focused on a notice board.

"God in heaven, I can think of plenty, and for good reason."

"Ingrid!" said Veronica with a gasp. "That's an awful thing to say!"

"Is it? And she was an awful person!"

3

"Ingrid, please!"

"Oh, come on, Veronica! You English, you are all the same! Why do you always do it?"

"Do what, Ingrid?"

"You know, whenever anyone dies – they immediately become wonderful people!" By this time she had turned around, and was leaning over the office counter, her piercing eyes meeting Veronica's. "Let us be honest, eh? She was a bitch, a troublemaker. She delighted in stirring up trouble."

"Ingrid, that's a dreadful thing to say!"

"It may be, but it's the truth. Causing trouble was like a hobby with her – just as most people decide which wine to drink or what to watch on the telly, so she decided whose life she could make a misery! It turned her on, I'm sure it did. It's what she lived for."

"Ingrid!"

"It's true. Are you going to deny it? Do you know, I'm quite sure she would wake up every morning and think about who she was going to get at and how she was going to do it."

"Well, there was one thing about her, she was always very efficient at her job," said Rosemary.

"So were Hitler and Franco," said Mick O'Reilly.

"Mick! We're talking about a dead colleague!"

He held up a hand. "Yes, yes, I know we are, Rosemary. I know what you mean. But I do have to say that I know what Ingrid's saying. For a start, Delia wasn't a colleague."

"What are you saying?"

"Delia wasn't a colleague, Veronica. Not in the true sense of the word. She might have worked in the same place as us, yes, but she was no colleague."

"Oh, Mick, come on."

He shrugged. "It's all right for you, Veronica, she wasn't in the Sociology section, she was in the English section. You didn't have to work closely with her like Paul and I had to. It was a nightmare, at times, I'm telling you."

"But surely you could speak to her?"

"Speak to her? About what? I never had a conversation with the woman in my life. Have you? Not what you'd call a real conversation. None of us have,

4

I'll bet. All she could ever talk about was the time-table, or a room clash, or who got what wrong on some memo or handout. It was like dealing with a robot."

"Worse than a robot, I would think," said Ingrid Kaltz, nodding slowly. "At least robots don't go out of their way to upset people."

"They think we are all robots! They couldn't give a piss about us!"

Mick O'Reilly couldn't help but grin on hearing the voice of another person who had just come into the office. He turned around to find Jean-Luc Lafarge looking flustered. Jean-Luc, as well as crucifying English idioms, was always at pains to point out that he was Belgian and not French, despite earning his living as a member of the French section.

"Who do, Jean-Luc?" asked Rosemary Hepworth.

"The so-called management here! They think we are all robots! Then they shit on us from high up, with the fan on!"

"Jean-Luc,…" Veronica Makepeace began.

"Before you say anything, yes, I am late," the Belgian shouted. "I suppose the students will have gone by now. They wait ten seconds, then they piss off to the coffee bar. Then they will complain about me, like they always do. They sit there hoping I don't come, then complain if I don't. It wasn't my fault – I had trouble with the buggering car on the motorway, and had to stop on the cold shoulder."

"Jean-Luc, Delia is dead."

The Belgian pushed his glasses further up the bridge of his nose and stared at Ingrid Kaltz.

"Mon Dieu! I wish she was!"

Rosemary started wailing again from behind her PC, Veronica tut-tutting at Jean-Luc.

"Jean-Luc, you haven't understood me." Ingrid put her face nearer his, and spoke slowly and loudly, like a British tourist abroad. "Listen to what I am saying. Delia is dead. Murdered."

He held up his hands. "What? Where? It wasn't me – I swear. I've just been on the motorway, waiting for the RAF."

"RAC, Jean-Luc."

"That's what I said, didn't I?"

"Ah, Paul, can I have a word?" said Mick O'Reilly to a tall, dark-haired man

5

in his early thirties who was walking past the office. Paul Richardson was one of Mick's colleagues in the English section, and was about to complete his first year at the College. He was a very capable member of staff, conscientious and organised, and he and Mick had got on well from the first day of his appointment.

Mick took him to one side in the corridor, lowering his voice as he spoke. "It's about Delia, Paul…"

"Oh, right, Mick. What's she gone and done now? It's only Monday morning, and she's done something already?" Paul's head turned towards the other end of the corridor, where Delia's office was situated. His eyes narrowed as he noticed that a couple of security men were standing outside it. "What's happened, Mick?"

Mick led him to a corner in the corridor. "Well, you're not going to believe this, Paul, but she's been murdered." He nodded, as a way of underlining what he had said. "Yes. Done in. Here, in her office."

"What? When?"

"This morning some time. Anne Dickinson found her. Poor girl, she's the nervous type at the best of times. I suppose one of us should see her. She'll need counselling."

Paul's eyes were still shocked. "And Delia's husband… Does he know?"

"I don't know, Paul. I know I shouldn't say it, but I don't think it was a marriage made in heaven anyway. I think he was more interested in running his business and making money than in anything else." He sighed. "You're right, though. He should be told, if he doesn't know already. Mind you, God knows where he'll be. I think he's away on business more than he's at home."

Paul was staring at his colleague. "Another murder, Mick. You know, the lad you told me about who was a student here…"

"Yes, I was thinking that. Poor Michael Springer, yes, graduated a couple of years ago. And now Delia."

Mick was about to say something else when a car stopped right by the main door of the building, two police cars screeching to a halt behind it. ⸱

Detective-Inspector Ray Farrar was never at ease with the academic life. For a start, he had never really experienced it, shunning the opportunity to go to university on obtaining three respectable A Level passes and choosing instead to follow in his father's footsteps and join the police. That had been almost thirty years ago, and since that time he had risen steadily through the ranks, the result of hard work and a keen analytical mind.

Besides his children's entry into university, his only first-hand experience of the academic life had been a few years ago. At that time he worked in another force and had been invited to give a talk on the police and the community at the students' union at the University of the North Midlands. Although most of the audience had been polite and well behaved, there had been a substantial minority who seemingly had no desire to listen or to engage in meaningful discussion, and who had interrupted many of his answers with jeers and catcalls. But what was to shock and depress him even more, he was to find out later, was that one or two of the academic staff had actually condoned such behaviour.

He took his eyes off the hypnotic movement of the windscreen wipers and turned to his colleague.

"So your next-door neighbour teaches at the College, then, Mark?"

His driver, recently promoted Detective-Sergeant Mark Newport, had given him this bit of information when news of the murder had come in.

"That's right, sir. His name's Paul Richardson. A very nice bloke."

"What does he teach?"

"English, sir. English language and literature. The same as the murdered woman."

"Well, well, that's interesting. From the same department, or section, or whatever... He could be a most valuable source of inside information on the victim and on the place in general. How well do you know him?"

"Oh, quite well, sir. His wife – her name's Helen - had their third child the same time as Julie had Lauren. She's a teacher as well, a primary school teacher, like Julie - or was, until the kids came. Julie got to know her quite well, as they had their job in common and were going to antenatal classes together. And their second one goes to the same playgroup as Aidan, so they see a lot of each other. We've got to know each other through the children, really."

Ray Farrar smiled. "Yes, been there, Mark. God, it seems like only yesterday.

And now I'm about to be a grandfather." He adjusted his sitting position in an attempt to stretch his long legs. "So you know the guy who's the lecturer quite well, then?"

"Well, we've been round to each other's house a few times for a meal, we have a chat out in the garden, that sort of thing, sir. But he tends not to talk much about his work." He pulled a face. "Mind you, I suppose I don't, unless I'm with another policeman, and then of course you end up talking shop."

Ray Farrar laughed. "Tell me about it!"

"The only time Paul's really talked about work at any length was a month or so ago, when someone was found murdered somewhere near Manchester. He'd been a student at the College a couple of years ago, before Paul was teaching there, so Paul didn't know him. But he said a lot of people at the College who had known him were upset when the news of it came out."

The inspector's brown eyes narrowed in thought. "Oh, yes, that case. They're still working on it, I believe. No real suspect yet found. And he used to be a student at the College, eh?"

"You're not thinking of the possibility of a link, sir?"

Ray Farrar laughed. "I think that there are possibilities for everything, Mark!" He shook his head. "A murder as far away as Manchester? No, I don't think so. But, like I said, you never know. Strange that two people connected to the same college are bumped off in quite a short space of time. Anyway, about the College... A C of E place, isn't it?"

"Not any longer, sir, not really. It used to be for C of E students, and was run by the Church, but I think those links aren't as strong as they used to be. I think there are still a few vicars on the board of governors, though, and the chairman is the Archdeacon of Parkdale."

"Oh, right. It's got a decent reputation, or certainly used to have."

Mark Newport nodded. "That's right, sir. From what my neighbour says, it's trying to get university status."

"Anything else you know about the place, Mark?"

"Well, Paul always speaks warmly about his immediate boss, Mick, I think his name is. A scouser." He gave a little laugh. "There's something else, as well, sir."

"Go on."

. "Well, I know it sounds like gossip, but there was one interesting thing about the College that Paul's wife said to Julie a few weeks ago, sir, when they were having a coffee together."

Ray Farrar turned to face his colleague as the main building of Parkdale College came into view, his eyes fired with a keen interest.

"Oh. What was that, then, Mark?"

"Well, she said that some of her husband's colleagues are very nice, easy to chat to and get on with…"

"And?"

"Well, she also said that, where some of the others are concerned, she's never met a bigger bunch of nutcases in her life."

Chapter 2

Helen Richardson had taken her eldest son to school before going into town with her other two children. She had just got off the bus in the town centre, and had just thanked an elderly man for carrying the folded push-chair from the bus for her, when she saw a familiar figure on the other side of the road. She snorted with derision when she saw him going into a betting shop.

"Isn't that man one of the people daddy works with, mummy?"

She looked down at her three-year old son and smiled. "Yes, that's right, Thomas. Fancy you noticing that."

"He was going into that shop the other day, as well."

"Was he, now?"

"Yes. Why isn't he at work, like daddy is?"

Out of the mouths of babes, she thought grimly. "I don't know, darling. Doing his research, I suppose," she said, partly to herself.

She was about to wheel her youngest son into a shoe shop while ushering in Thomas, when she recognised a tall, thin man with shrunken eyes on his way out.

"Jim, how are you?"

"Hello, Helen. Nice to see you." He looked down at the children. "See you've got the tribe with you!"

She nodded and smiled. "Well, part of the tribe – I've just taken James to school. Er, anyway, how's Edith?"

"Not too good. You know, it's only a matter of time, really…"

She touched his arm. "Jim, you mustn't give up hope. I know it's easy saying that…"

"No, you're right, Helen." The man tried to give a tight smile, nodding his head vigorously. "And how's Paul? Still surviving in the madhouse?"

"That sums it up perfectly, Jim. If he didn't have Mick there, I don't know what he'd do."

"I can imagine. He's a great bloke, is Mick. He was fantastic when I told him about Edith."

"Yes, I'm sure he was. He always makes out he's the light-hearted comedian, but deep down he really cares about people. Paul loves working with him."

Jim Gregory, who had taught French at the College, had taken early retirement at Christmas when he and his wife had discovered how ill she was. Like Mick O'Reilly, he had gone out of his way to be helpful to Paul when he had first joined the staff, and Helen had never forgotten that.

"I've just seen the Assistant Head of Department at one of his places of research," she said, trying to cheer him up.

He gave a knowing smile. "Eric Fisher? Where, on the golf course or in the betting shop?"

She laughed. "Right with the second one!" She shook her head. "And he's only been at the College two terms! Honestly, Jim, how does he get away with it?"

"Simply because he knows that Cassidy won't do a thing about it, Helen. That's one of the main reasons why the department's in such a shambles – as well as having a gang of nutters there, too, of course, though I don't mean everyone when I say that."

"He's also got the gift of the gab, which helps."

"Oh, yes. He could sell condoms in the Vatican. Aren't they all the same, though, those on their way up the greasy pole? That's why I admire people like Mick so much – he's always refused to be part of it."

"Well, from what Paul says, he actually takes the mickey out of it, which I suppose doesn't go down well with those high up."

"Well, Mick has higher priorities than sucking up to idiots. He's a great teacher, and I think the students know that he does his best for them. A pity there aren't more like him."

"Yes, Paul says he's lovely to work with. Kind and human. A bit of a comedian, as well."

"That's right, that's Mick summed up perfectly. He'd do anything for anyone. He tries to hide it, of course, with his brash sense of humour."

"Anyway, Jim, I won't keep you," she said hurriedly as she saw him steal a glance at his watch.

"Oh, no, it's OK, Helen, don't worry. Edith's sister's staying for a few days, and the girls are coming up tomorrow."

"Oh, that's nice, Jim. It'll be nice company for Edith, and it also takes the pressure off you a bit."

"You're right. Anyway, tell Paul to take it easy, eh?"

"Oh, he's too conscientious for his own good."

He shook his head and gave a sad smile. "I'm telling you, Helen, the more you do in that place, they worse you make it for yourself. When I think of the years I spent there, lying awake at night almost worrying myself sick about stupid meetings invented for no real reason at all, where nasty idiots just wanted to put the knife into others and draw attention to themselves..."

"Yes, Paul says that half of the time all these meetings that crop up are nothing but a type of stage that certain people want to perform on."

"Exactly, Helen. The place seems to have the worst of both worlds. You wouldn't mind if it was totally disorganised but had warmth, or if it had no warmth but was efficient. But it has neither. And I used to take it so seriously and worry about it, but saying nothing in case I upset someone. I must have been mad..."

"You can't help how you're made, though, Jim... What worries me is, I think Paul's the same..."

"Oh, he is, Helen. The same as Mick. Edith used to tell me repeatedly that I worked too hard, worried too much, took the job and the place too seriously. And what happened when I retired? I didn't even get a note of thanks from any of the suit-and-clipboard brigade, as Mick calls them. Not a note of thanks."

"No, Jim – but you got the respect and affection of people like Mick and the students. And that's what counts. I wonder how many of the suit-and-clipboard brigade can say that they get Christmas cards from people they taught years and years ago?"

The woman shook hands with both policemen. "I'm Amy Richmond. I'm the nurse at the student health centre here."

She was a little overweight, of medium height, and had a ruddy complexion and kind eyes. Everything about her seemed maternal and caring. Ray Farrar put her in her early to mid fifties.

"I know that this must be an awful shock for a young student, nurse

Richmond. But there are a few questions we want to ask her. We'll be as tactful as we can, and it won't take more than a few minutes. We would be grateful if you could be with her, if that's all right."

The interview was indeed very short. Anne Dickinson sat next to the nurse, her shoulders hunched as if she was trying to make her body go as small as possible. Her face was white, her eyes wide and tear-filled as she played repeatedly with her long dark hair. She had very little to tell, in that she had been in Dr Bumstead's office no more than ten seconds, if that. When she began to describe the precise moment when she realised her English lecturer had met such an awful death, her body began to shake and she clung to the nurse like an infant would to its mother.

"We may need to see you again sometime, in the course of our enquiries, nurse Richmond," said Ray Farrar as they were about to leave the health centre.

"Of course, inspector." She produced a card.

He nodded in the direction of the room where they had left the student. "And thank you for your help." He glanced at a notice board near the door, giving details of when the nurse was available for student consultation. "You must be very busy, nurse Richmond."

She smiled and nodded. "Yes. Especially when the exam period starts to draw near. And many of them have part-time jobs as well, to make ends meet. Being a student is no easy option these days. They have more pressures on them than people think."

She left them at the door, giving brief instructions on the shortest route to take to the main building, then returned to comfort Anne Dickinson.

"Good morning, I'm Dr Harold Cassidy, Head of Department."

As the inspector shook hands with the man, the thought of cold fish on a slab somehow came to mind. From the look on his D.S.'s face, it was obvious that his reaction was more or less the same.

"I've informed the staff, inspector – well, those that are here."

The inspector eyed him cautiously, a rotund man with a red fleshy face. "Does that mean that there are some staff who aren't here?"

Harold Cassidy rubbed his flabby hands together and smiled as one would to a trying child. "Oh, yes. Some staff are engaged on research, you see. They tend to do that at home."

"And have all the staff been contacted?"

"Yes, all the staff have been notified – Rosemary, the secretary, has managed to contact everyone who isn't here, or has left messages for them."

"I see. Well, I want to address all the staff before my colleague and I start interviewing them individually."

The man's eyes were immediately concerned. "Individually?"

"Yes, Dr Cassidy. This is a murder enquiry. I know it must be an awful shock for everyone."

"Yes, terrible, terrible. I was just thinking, it's going to play havoc with next year's time-table."

"I beg your pardon?"

"Next year's time-table, inspector." The man grimaced at the thought. "Delia's death is going to cause a lot of inconvenience."

Ray Farrar exchanged a glance with Mark Newport, then quickly said, "Oh, I see." He looked at his watch and thought for a few seconds. "Fine, shall we say in a quarter of an hour's time in the largest room available? In the meantime, I'd like to have Dr Bumstead's file, please."

"Her file?"

"Yes. I assume the department keeps staff records?"

"Oh, yes, but they contain all sorts of personal information, and I wouldn't like the staff to think-"

"Dr Cassidy, with the greatest respect, what staff think about us looking at their files is irrelevant. This is a murder enquiry."

The man swallowed, then nodded his head repeatedly. "Of course, inspector. It's just that, well, certain staff have very strong feelings about things like personal files."

The inspector's unblinking eyes met his. "Then they are welcome to share their strong feelings with me, Dr Cassidy." He gave the hint of a smile. "Dr Bumstead's file, please?"

Seconds later, Rosemary Hepworth, who was the first person that the policemen had met on arrival, and still looking red-eyed, flustered and nervous, opened a large filing cabinet and handed a dark green file to the inspector.

Then she turned to the Head of Department. "Harold, I think everyone's here now. Well, everyone except Eric, but I've paged him, so he should be on his way."

Harold Cassidy nodded. "OK, thanks, Rosemary. Perhaps we could all go to LT1."

"LT1?"

"Lecture Theatre 1, inspector." The condescending half smile implied that the question was a silly one.

"Fine, Dr Cassidy." Ray Farrar gestured to the file that he had handed on to Mark Newport. "Just give us a quarter of an hour, please."

"Anne, you've got to go home. You can't stay here." Geraldine Murphy's eyes earnestly surveyed her friend as they sat down in a corner of the student bar.

Anne Dickinson played for a few seconds with a ring on her right hand. "I'll be all right. I don't want to go home, it's best if I stay here with you lot. Besides, I've got to go to work tonight."

"Go to work? How can you go to work after what you've been through today?"

"Geraldine, I've got no choice. I need the money. It's OK for you, your family's quite well off." She touched her friend's arm. "Oh, I didn't mean it like that. You know what I mean."

"I know, I know..."

"It's impossible to manage otherwise. I've got no choice but to earn a bit of money. My mum and dad do their best, but they can't give me all that much. My dad's working overtime as it is." She snorted. "What was the phrase again – *Education, education, education.* Don't make me laugh! When I finish the course, I'll be in debt for life, I think."

"When's your first exam?"

Anne thought for a second. "What day is it? God, my mind's gone blank since this morning." She took a gulp of coffee. "A fortnight tomorrow – French translation."

"Are you sure you'll be OK?"

"Yeah, I'll be all right." She turned to her friend and tried to laugh. "I tell you what, the Carlsberg'll go down well tonight!"

"What do you mean, tonight? We can always start at lunchtime!" Geraldine tried to laugh, but merely shook her head. "God, what are we saying? Delia Bumstead's dead – murdered. I know she wasn't everyone's favourite person, but…"

"I know what you mean. Most of the staff didn't like her, did they?"

"Well, I think some of them hated her guts. I tell you what, I wouldn't mind being a fly on the wall in the staff common room right now…"

"Right, Mark, not an awful lot to go on, is there?" The inspector studied the notes he had made from the victim's personal file. "Forty-two years of age, married, no children. Worked here for fifteen years. BA and PhD from the University of Cumbria… Written articles on various subjects. Hold on… She took four years to complete her degree. That's strange."

"What's that, sir?"

"My daughter's English degree was only a three-year course. I wonder why she took an extra year…" He closed the file. "OK Mark, let's meet her esteemed colleagues."

A couple of minutes later, the two policemen were in a large and well-lit lecture theatre with rows of gently rising seats.

"OK, everybody, can I please introduce you to Detective Inspector … er…"

"Farrar," said the policeman to the Head of Department. "And this is Detective Sergeant Newport." The inspector noticed that Harold Cassidy had to clap his hands in an attempt to attract his colleagues' attention, and that even then some of his colleagues failed to take any notice of him.

"Can we have some hush, please?"

The question was put, in a loud clear voice, by a tall well-built man in his late forties. He had black hair parted down the middle, which reminded the inspector of old cigarette cards of footballers from the 1950s era.

There was immediate silence.

"Er, thank you, Terry," said Dr Cassidy.

The man called Terry surveyed the scene as if he was the owner of the place. He nodded at the inspector in an unspoken way of stating that he could now speak without fear of interruption, then slowly sat down. It was then that Mark Newport spotted Paul Richardson, his neighbour, who was sitting in the front row and who gave him a slight nod as a sign of acknowledgement. He also thought that Paul had given him the slightest of winks.

"Now, as I was saying-"

The door was suddenly pushed open and a tall, tanned man in his mid to late forties and wearing an expensive-looking suit appeared.

"Sorry to be late, Harold. I was just doing some research."

"On the 3.15 at Haydock Park," murmured a man sitting next to Paul Richardson, in a Liverpool accent. Mark Newport presumed he was his next-door neighbour's colleague in the English section.

"Oh, that's all right, Eric. Take a seat."

The Head of Department beamed around the room. "OK, everyone-"

"Harold, was it really necessary to drag us all in so early in the morning?"

The speaker was of medium height, with shoulder length dark hair, and was wearing a denim jacket and matching jeans. A young woman with frizzy hair sitting next to him made noises of agreement and clapped vigorously.

The man sitting next to Paul Richardson who had made the comment about Haydock Park turned around and grinned.

"What's wrong, Dominic? Did you have to come in a bit earlier from your Marxist-Leninist five-bedroom detached?"

The man's eyes blazed. "And don't you live in a detached house?"

"I do, Dominic. But I do try to make sure there isn't much of a gap between what I preach and how I live."

The man in denim pointed a finger. "When the abused proletariat awaken from their sleep of brainwashing-"

"Yes, yes, Dominic. We've heard it all before."

"You're a traitor to your class!"

"No, Dominic – on the contrary, I've done what everyone from my class background wants to do: I've managed to make a more decent life for myself and my family. But you can't see that." He looked at the man and shook his head. "What in God's name does someone from your background know about the working classes?"

"I know all about the working classes!"

"Of course you do, Dominic. You've read books on them."

The man called Terry got up from his chair again. "Like I said, can we have some hush, please? Can I remind you all that someone in the next building is lying dead?" He jutted his head towards the man called Dominic. "I would have thought that any time of the day wouldn't be too early for a meeting, in such circumstances!"

Dominic turned to face him. "All this has disturbed my Monday morning routine. It's most inconvenient, having to come in so early!"

Ray Farrar glanced at his watch and then at Dominic. "I'm sorry, your name is…?"

"Carruthers."

"Well, Mr Carruthers…"

"*Dr* Carruthers, actually."

"Oh, I do beg your pardon."

"Surely it doesn't matter about your title, does it, Dominic?" said the man with the Merseyside accent, a smirk on his face. "I mean, we're all equal, aren't we – or so you keep telling us."

"Dr Carruthers," Ray Farrar went on, "with the greatest of respect, I wouldn't call half past ten in the morning early."

Dominic Carruthers stood up again, and addressed his colleagues, his eyes staring and arms outstretched. "Do you see, everyone? Do you see what would happen if these people" - he pointed towards the two policemen – "if these people were to come to power? Do you see what would happen in a police state? We would be the hapless victims of state-sponsored harassment!"

The man with the scouse accent turned around again. "Oh, shut up Dominic, give it a rest. I don't know what world people like you live in. My father had to leave the house every morning at seven o'clock, and came back every night at seven o'clock absolutely knackered. As Terry's said, there's someone who's lying dead, murdered, for Christ's sake." He then turned to Ray Farrar. "Sorry, officer, do go on."

Ray Farrar smiled and nodded. "Thank you." Then he stood up. "All staff will be interviewed throughout the day, by Detective-Sergeant Newport and me, along with two other colleagues. A time-table will be drawn up within the next hour." He turned to the secretary. "Mrs Hepworth, I'd be obliged if that could be done…"

She nodded silently.

"Does this also mean that lectures are cancelled, Inspector?" asked the tanned man who had come in late. As though reading the inspector's thoughts, he added, "I'm Dr Fisher, by the way, Eric Fisher, Assistant Head of Department." He smiled at each of the policemen, his eyes becoming slits. "It's just that I'm concerned about all this interfering with the work schedule."

Mark Newport noticed that his next-door neighbour and the man with the scouse accent had to stifle a laugh at this.

"I see, thank you. In answer to your question, yes, in the present circumstances I feel it is best that teaching is cancelled. However, I want all staff to be available throughout the day." He tried not to look at Dominic Carruthers. "And I wish to stress that that means the whole day."

As he and Mark Newport were leaving the lecture theatre, followed by the staff, the inspector took the secretary to one side.

"Mrs Hepworth, I assume you also keep files on students, as well as staff?"

"Yes, inspector, we do. We keep them in the office." The eyes, while no longer reddened, were still puffy.

"Fine. I believe you used to have a student here who was murdered a few months ago?"

She nodded, her eyes again betraying emotion. "Yes, Michael Springer… He graduated a couple of years ago."

"Could I possibly see his file, too, please?"

Chapter 3

"What's going on, then?"

A few seconds elapsed before Ray Farrar realised that the question from someone in the milling crowd of students outside the building where Delia Bumstead's body had been found was being addressed to him. As the first person to see the body had been a student, he knew that the news would have spread like wildfire throughout the campus. So he had no alternative but to answer as best he could.

"A member of staff has been found dead. And we are treating it as a suspicious death."

"Hah! Suspicious, you say, when she's had her skull battered in!"

He quickly surveyed the young man in front of him. "And you are…?"

"I'm Nigel Jevons, the next president of the student union." He somehow said the words as though the policeman should have known who he was without asking.

He was of medium height, with dark lank hair which touched the collar of his leather jacket. He had a goatee beard, and was thin and nervy, his body continually in motion. He folded his arms and scrutinised the policeman, peering at him with truculent eyes through expensive-looking glasses.

"It is murder, isn't it?"

"At this stage of the proceedings, we have an open mind."

"An open mind? Hah! Don't make me laugh! You can't fool me!"

Ray Farrar was beginning to dislike the young man more and more by the second. "Were you one of Dr Bumstead's students?"

"Yes, I was. And what I want to know is, when are they going to get a replacement?"

"A replacement?"

"For Dr Bumstead. Who's going to take over her lectures? Our education can't be allowed to suffer, can it? Don't you know that our parents are paying an awful lot of money for our education?"

The policeman refrained from saying that, with a daughter in her final year at university, he knew only too well, having just paid the second instalment of the contribution towards her fees.

"Do I hear you saying that you're very concerned about missing lectures because of Dr Bumstead's death, Nigel?"

The speaker was a small, slim woman, near retirement age in the policeman's estimation, who was smiling at the student knowingly.

"Yes, Maureen, that is precisely what I am saying!"

"I see. Well, well, that is nice to know, especially in view of what your attendance at everyone's lectures has been like for the past two years! Colleagues will be delighted to hear of your late conversion!"

He was momentarily stunned. "Er, well, I've been on student union business, that's why. It's a big responsibility, you know. The student union is a focal point of college life."

"And so are lectures, Nigel."

"But I'm standing for president of the students' union!"

"Of course, Nigel, forgive me, I forgot. It can't be easy, trying to be a student while playing at being one at the same time "

"What do you mean?"

"Well, Nigel, as someone who is possibly the next union president, you're a very important person."

"Exactly."

As Nigel Jevons turned away to harangue someone else, the woman turned to Ray Farrar and smiled, holding out her hand.

"Hello, I'm Maureen Threlfall. I teach History." She had candid blue eyes and a quiet yet somehow arresting voice, clear and precise, with a slight Scottish accent. She turned her head in Nigel Jevons's direction, and said even more quietly, "Pompous little sod. Full of himself, always has been. Ruined by mummy and daddy, probably. Knows his rights – a pity he doesn't know a tenth as much about his responsibilities."

The policeman immediately warmed to the woman. "Yes, I got that impression right away. But then again, maybe I thought I knew it all when I was that age."

"Perhaps, but I bet your parents had brought you up to speak to people properly."

He smiled and nodded, his mind in the past for a couple of seconds. "Yes, you're right."

She glanced at Nigel Jevons again. "They just haven't been told how to speak to people, some of these kids. Not all of them are like that, of course. A lot of them are lovely. But people like him over there are a pain in the backside. Call me old-fashioned, but I can't help thinking that this informal first-name business doesn't help. It makes people like Nigel Jevons think that they know at least as much as you do, if not more. I suppose it doesn't happen in your job, though."

He thought for a while. "Well it's creeping in. By the way, who's down to interview you?"

"You are, Mr Farrar. At half three. The interviews are to be in our own offices, aren't they?"

"That's right."

"Good. Are you a tea or coffee man?"

He smiled again. "Coffee. Milk and no sugar, please. But there'll be two of us. And he's awkward, he's a tea man."

"I can cope with that. When you've been in this place for more than twenty years, you learn to cope with almost anything!"

"Hi, Anne. Are you all right?"

Anne Dickinson turned away from the group of students she was with to find Mick O'Reilly standing over her.

"Oh, hello, Mick. Yes, I think I'm all right now. I've seen nurse Richmond. She had a chat with me and gave me something to help me sleep tonight." She pointed to a large brandy in front of her. "And this lot have gone and bought me this."

He grinned at the students who were seated around the table. "An excellent idea! My Irish grand-dad always used to say, in times of crisis, have a drink and say a prayer!" He looked around the student bar, then said, "Look, Anne, if you want to stay with your pals for the rest of the day, that's fine. But if you want to chat about things, you know where my office is."

"Thanks, Mick. I've already had a reporter here from the local paper, would you believe. News doesn't half get around fast!"

"What did he say to you?"

"She. She asked me how I'd come to find Delia, how I reacted, what sort of person she was, that sort of thing. Then she said she was off to try and find Dr Cassidy or Dr Fisher."

"Oh, God, you can do without being hassled by the press." He tore a thin strip off some advertising blurb that was lying on the next table and scribbled on it. "That's my home phone number. Ring me if you need to."

She gave a tight smile, tears not very far away. "Thanks, Mick, I appreciate that. Maureen Threlfall's just been in here, as well, and said I can see her whenever I want." Her eyes suddenly opened wide. "And Terry Trotter. He was really nice. I was absolutely gobsmacked."

Mick O'Reilly nodded his head and laughed. "Ah, Terry's got a heart of gold, really. He's just very good at hiding it. He's OK, deep down."

"He was really nice this morning. I used to be terrified of him when I was in the first year. In fact, most students still are!"

"And not just the students!"

He left the bar, feeling pleased that she was laughing.

"Hi, it's me. I've been trying to phone you."

Helen Richardson pulled a face as she held the telephone in one hand and tried to entice her youngest son to take some food with the other. "Oh, sorry, I forgot to take the mobile with me when I went into town." She frowned into the mouthpiece. "Are you OK?"

"Well, you're not going to believe this."

"Oh no, what is it? What on earth's happened in that place now?"

"It's Delia Bumstead..."

"Now there's a surprise!"

"No, listen, Helen. She's been murdered."

"What?" Her screech was loud enough to startle the child, who started crying. She put down the spoon and held him to her. "God, where... how?

"She was found this morning in her office, hit over the head with something. A student found her. She's been getting counselling."

"The poor girl. So, are the police there?"

"Yes. Funnily enough, Mark is here with them. He came with some inspector called Farrar, who spoke to all of us. We're all going to be interviewed, so heaven knows when I'll be back home tonight."

"OK, don't worry about that. God, isn't it awful? Julie's here now, actually. She's stopping for lunch with the kids. I'll tell her what's happened. Grief, what a place, eh? I'm starting to believe that anything can happen there. I saw Fisher in town this morning. He was going into a betting shop, large as life."

"Typical. God knows how he manages to get away with it. Anyway, I've got to go. I'll ring you if anything else happens."

She replaced the receiver and started stirring the baby food just as Julie Newport was coming down the stairs from the toilet, where she had been with her daughter.

"Julie, just wait till you hear this…"

The room was quite small, but with a high ceiling, and looked out onto a grassy expanse leading to distant hills dotted with sheep. The two police officers looked at the list of members of staff of the Department of Social and Language Studies that Rosemary Hepworth had typed out. As Ray Farrar had asked, she had also typed in the internal phone numbers and grouped the staff under the various academic subjects that they taught. Mark Newport had in his hand a page bearing the photographs of all the staff, academic and administrative, that Ray Farrar had asked for as a means of identification.

"Right, Mark. Let's look at the section your neighbour's in, English. There's your neighbour Paul Richardson, Dr Mick O'Reilly, who's the head of section, and the deceased."

Mark Newport's finger pointed to the bottom of the page. "There seem to be three part-time staff as well, sir, and one of them works in the English section – Mrs Frances McAteer."

"Yes, well spotted, Mark. I wonder if all the part-time staff were at the meeting this morning? There's only one way to find out." Ray Farrar reached across and dialled the secretary's internal number.

Seconds later, he put the phone down, having been informed that there were only three part-timers, and that all of them had attended the meeting.

"Right, Mark. I've allocated half an hour for each person. You and I are doing the English section, the French section and the History section. So, the English section: that's Dr O'Reilly, your neighbour, and the part-timer called Frances McAteer." He scanned a sheet of paper. "French – that's Dr Trotter, Jean-Luc Lafarge, and Liz Goodwin, who's also part-time. History – that's Mrs Threlfall, Ingrid Kaltz and a part-timer called Harriet Bond. The secretary will have to be interviewed, as well."

"That's going to keep us busy, sir. Do you hope to have all that done by today?"

"If we can. No doubt some moaning bugger will complain about being kept here all hours, as they see it. But that's too bad." He consulted the sheet again. "Now, where was I? Yes, Gillian Taylor and Alan Henry are on their way, they should be here at any minute. They can do the Geography section – Gillian'll soon sort out that stroppy bugger preaching about class warfare – what's his name again?"

"Carruthers, Dominic Carruthers."

"*Dr* Dominic Carruthers, don't forget! Geography, yes… someone called Susan Barrow, as well. And Gillian and Alan are also doing the Sociology section. Sociology – Veronica Makepeace and a Lucinda Hobbs-Smithers."

"And the Head of Department and his assistant, sir?"

Ray Farrar tapped his pad with his pen. "Aye, we'll do them as well. As bad as each other, aren't they, if you ask me. It seems to me the Head of Department couldn't care less, deep down. Did you notice how many times he actually yawned during the meeting this morning? We were talking about one of his staff being murdered, and he just didn't give a toss, as far as I could see."

"That was another thing that Helen, Paul's wife, always says, sir. She says that many of them seem remote, wrapped up in their own little world. You know, they could tell you who was King of France in 1700 but they wouldn't know who David Beckham was."

"Or worse than that," said the inspector raising a finger, "I bet that some of them are so bloody affected that they'd *pretend* they didn't know who David Beckham was."

"And the Assistant Head, sir?" Mark Newport was quite sure that his boss's assessment of the man would be the same as his, especially in view of the sarcastic comment about the 3.15 at Haydock Park by the man with the scouse accent.

"Well, his type are everywhere, aren't they? Glib, plausible, clever with the patter. Street-wise. An educated Arthur Daley. You wouldn't trust him with your mother-in-law. Probably walks around with a pencil behind his ear while talking in a loud voice, but in actual fact does bugger all."

Mark Newport changed position in his chair. "Certainly, from what Paul Richardson and his wife say occasionally, especially after a drink or two, what you say about them both is spot on, sir."

The inspector rubbed his chin. "How do you feel about interviewing your neighbour? Comfortable with it?"

"Oh, yes, sir. Paul will know there's a job to be done, and he'll be as helpful as he can."

"Good." Ray Farrar stretched in his chair. "God, we've only been here a few hours, and it's already obvious that there's an interesting variety of characters, to put it mildly. Mind you, I suppose you'll have known that already through chatting to Paul Richardson."

Mark Newport nodded. "I remember Paul saying one evening, after he'd had a few down him, that the trouble with this place is that there are people here who deserve to be paid twice their salary, and there are people who'd be overpaid at twenty quid a week."

"Aye. Name me any job where that isn't the case…"

"It's awful, Helen. Paul will be in a right state. I hope Mark goes easy with him!"

"Well, nothing about that place could shock me, really, Julie. But I must admit, this beats everything. I mean, I know that teaching in a primary school's stressful, where you've got pushy parents who are convinced that their little darling can do no wrong."

"Or that if their little darling isn't making enough progress then it must be your fault, because it will have said so in one of the tabloids."

"Exactly. But there's a camaraderie in teaching, as well, isn't there? That's what Paul says he misses about school teaching, the laugh that you can have in the staff room. At the College, well, a lot of them just seem so remote."

"There are some nice people there, though, aren't there?"

"Oh, yes. Mick, Paul's section leader, is great. Ingrid's nice, as well – she's a German girl who teaches European History. And there's Maureen, Maureen Threlfall, though she's retiring soon. And Terry Trotter's OK."

Julie was laughing. "Who?"

Helen found that the laughter was infectious. "Terry Trotter!"

"He sounds as though he should be in the *Dandy* or the *Beano*!"

"He's quite normal, actually. At least he knows there are other things in life besides Parkdale College. If he sees you, he'll chat to you and ask you how the kids are. That reminds me, do you know the school's going to have Ofsted coming?"

"What, the school here in the village, you mean?"

"Yes."

"I bet that'll please the staff. Who told you?"

"Sylvia, the secretary, this morning, when I was taking James to school."

"I bet you're glad you're missing that, Helen!"

"I certainly am. Sylvia also showed me the list of the names of those in the Ofsted team."

"One of the perks of being a former member of staff, eh?"

"Yes. The big cheese is someone called Allardyce, George Allardyce."

Julie Newport slowly put down her mug of coffee. Her eyes were wide open. "Not George Allardyce?" She shook her head. "Him – leading an Ofsted team. I don't believe it."

"Do you know him?"

"I taught with him, some years ago, when we lived in Yorkshire."

"What was he like?"

"Absolutely useless – the kids were taught virtually nothing, he could hardly control them, even seven year olds. But he was also absolutely full of himself. And absolutely half way up the backside of the Head and anyone else who could be useful. It was pathetic to watch. All the staff knew what sort of a teacher he

27

was, all the staff knew how he sucked up to the Head. But nothing was ever said. It's difficult, I suppose, to say anything in that sort of situation."

"And he's now in charge of an Ofsted visit?"

"Yes." She sighed and stared at the ceiling. "George Allardyce, who can't teach for toffee, who bores anyone and everyone in sight – especially kids in the classroom – is going to make other people's lives a misery for a week. People who can teach ten times better than he can. And the little sod will be strutting around, enjoying every minute of it, having the nerve to give advice to people who can do the job better than he ever could, and probably earning loads of money in the process. Ofsted! Hah! As if there isn't enough stress in the job already!"

"When you think of it, the country's gone mad, hasn't it?"

" Oh yes."

Chapter 4

"Thank you very much for all your help, Mrs Hepworth."

The secretary smiled awkwardly and brushed a hand through her hair. "Oh, that's my job, inspector. Pleased to be of help."

"Two of our colleagues will be interviewing you later in the afternoon. We hope we can do it before five o'clock – we don't want to detain you."

The two policemen had met the secretary by chance on their way back to the college buildings after a talk with some members of the forensic team outside the building where the body had been found.

"It's shorter this way," she said, indicating with a shaking hand a path between some secretive trees.

They had gone no further than twenty yards along the path when they heard voices. Two female voices. The two policemen glanced at each other and instinctively slowed down, as did Rosemary Hepworth.

Two women were standing in the middle of a thick clump of trees. One of them, overweight and squat, had her arm around the waist of the other, who was quite tall and thin. It was impossible for the police officers to hear what the women were saying without them being seen, but their tones and their body language – as well as the privacy of the spot - suggested that this was no ordinary conversation.

"Oh dear," said the secretary, with an embarrassed smile.

Ray Farrar smiled but said nothing, trying to see if he recognised the two women from the staff photographs that he had been given. He looked at the secretary, who immediately answered his unspoken question, holding her hands in a posture of prayer as she did so.

"It's, er, Harriet and Veronica." The inspector tried to put surnames to the two women. Rosemary Hepworth did it for him. "Harriet Bond and Veronica Makepeace. Harriet teaches History, she's a part-timer, and Veronica teaches Social Policy." At that very second, Harriet Bond's voice became loud and shrill.

"So you keep saying! And how can I believe you, when it happens time and time again?"

"Oh dear," said the secretary. "I think they're having one of their tiffs."

The two policemen exchanged a rapid glance, both appreciating the intimacy implied by the word.

"I see," said Ray Farrar.

Nothing else was said until they went into the building where the office was situated.

"OK, Mrs Hepworth, we'll see you later. And thank you for the file on the student called Springer."

The woman gave the inspector a nervous smile and disappeared into the ladies' toilet without saying a word.

"So we're the first to be interviewed, then, Paul."

Mick O'Reilly had just finished marking an essay. He sighed as he entered the mark in a register, then switched on an electric kettle and threw a spoonful of coffee into two mugs.

"I still can't believe it, Mick, I just can't. I wonder if it's someone here, or an outsider."

"It could be anyone. A member of staff, a student, a complete stranger – you know, some nutter who's wandered in from outside and attacked her for no reason at all."

"But if it's someone from here, what was the motive? It could be anything."

"Yes, exactly. It's an awful thing to say, but when you think of the sort of person she was, I bet she had more enemies than friends."

"Well, the only friend Delia had on the staff was Liz Goodwin, wasn't it? Nobody else got on with her."

"Yes, but I sometimes think Liz was only nice to her because she knew what Delia could be capable of. That's the main reason why she's always sided with her in staff meetings, that sort of thing. Unless there's something that we don't know about. Nothing would surprise me about this bloody place. Also, Liz has been wanting to become full-time for ages, and probably saw Delia as her one big ally because Delia had a thing about the status of part-timers." Mick poured the boiling water in the mugs. "Mind you, I think Delia had strong feelings about everything – growing tomatoes, keeping goldfish – you name it, she had strong feelings about it."

Suddenly the door burst open and a tall, slightly overweight young woman came in. She had sheets of paper in her hand.

"Oh, hello, Belinda. My hearing must be going. I didn't hear you knock," said Mick drily.

"I've got a complaint to make!" She waved the papers in front of him. He then realised that it was a piece of work that had been marked.

"And what's your complaint, Belinda?"

"It's about this essay that I did on Queen Victoria!"

The man smiled. "Yes, what about it?"

"Maureen Threlfall marked it-"

"Then why don't you see her about it?"

"Because you're the second year tutor. My parents have always told me to go to the top whenever you have a complaint."

"Have they now? You obviously have first-rate parents. And what's your complaint, Belinda? What terrible injustice has Mrs Threlfall perpetrated?"

The young woman screwed her face up in bewilderment. "Has she what?"

"Never mind, Belinda. What's Mrs Threlfall done?"

"She's only gone and given me fifty-five for this essay!"

"That's not bad…"

"Well, I think it should be sixty!"

He put down his mug of coffee and walked over to the window. "Come over here and have a look at my car, Belinda."

Paul Richardson, knowing his colleague's wicked sense of humour, grinned to himself, knowing that something was coming.

"What sort of car is it?"

She cast disdainful eyes over the vehicle. "It's an Astra."

He pointed to the mark of fifty-five written on her essay and then to the car. "And I think it should be a BMW."

"A tiff, eh, sir?"

Ray Farrar and Mark Newport were on their way to interview Mick O'Reilly and Paul Richardson.

31

"Aye, well, each to their own, as they say. Their relationship's their business, I suppose."

"What they were arguing about might be our business, though, sir."

"You could well be right, Mark. We'll find out soon enough. Anyway, let's go and see what Dr O'Reilly and your neighbour have to tell us."

Just then a tall broad-chested man in a grey suit strode imperiously towards them from the far end of the corridor. The swagger was openly confident as he held out his hand to the inspector.

"Bent."

Ray Farrar looked at the smiling face, beady eyes behind horn-rimmed glasses. "I beg your pardon?"

"Bent, Cuthbert Bent. Assistant Director, Personnel. You'll have heard of me."

"Of course," said the policeman, his younger colleague marvelling at how his superior had kept a straight face.

"Mr Feller, isn't it?"

"Farrar."

"Yes, quite." The man turned to Mark Newport, his ruddy face wreathed in a questioning smile.

"Detective Sergeant Newport."

"Yes, yes, of course. How do you do?" His voice dropped to a hissing whisper. "Terrible business, isn't it, about Delia what's-her-name? I knew her well, you know."

"Really?"

"Oh, yes. Well, in my position as Assistant Director for Personnel, it's my job, isn't it?"

"I see. Would you say that she got on well with her colleagues?"

The man nodded his head vigorously. "Oh, yes, yes. Delia was a very popular member of staff. Well, she always got on extremely well with those of us in upper management, anyway."

"Really?"

"Oh yes. Played a good game of badminton, too, you know, and always gave excellent dinner parties."

"I see..."

"Oh, yes, yes. She always had the good of the College at heart, too, you know. She was always an excellent source of important information on the workings of the department and its staff."

"I see. And besides upper management, how did she get on with the less important members of staff?"

Again, Mark Newport tried hard to look impassive.

"Ah, well, that's another story, inspector." The man rocked backwards and forwards as he solemnly considered the faults of those who were his inferiors. "She had no time for scivers, poor Delia. You see…" – at this he gave a sad world-weary smile – "there are people here who don't take the job seriously enough. They spend too much time worrying about the students."

"I beg your pardon?"

"You know, they don't pay enough attention to the important things to do with the job."

"Ah, I see," said Ray Farrar, giving his colleague the tiniest of nudges. "They spend too much time in the classroom and not enough time at meetings or producing paperwork."

The man held his arms out triumphantly.

"Exactly!" He looked at his watch. "Anyway, nice meeting you, Mr Feller, Mr Newbury. Must be off – I've got a highly important meeting to chair on the self-standing remit of interchangeable parameters."

And he was off, his heels echoing on the parquet floor.

"Mark, you know what Paul Richardson's wife said about the place?"

"Yes, sir?"

"Well, I admire her understatement."

Still laughing, they turned a corner into another corridor just in time to see a young woman with sheets of paper in her hand slam the door of the office that Mick O'Reilly shared with Paul Richardson. She stormed past them, red faced, almost bumping into them. The two men pulled a face at each other before Ray Farrar knocked on the door.

It was opened by Paul Richardson, who shook hands with the inspector.

"You two already know each other, of course," said Ray Farrar, tilting his head towards his colleague. The two neighbours grinned at each other, then the two policemen shook hands with Mick O'Reilly.

"Can I get you two gentleman a coffee, a tea, or anything?"

"Not for me, thanks, Dr O'Reilly." The D.S. also said no, with a polite shake of his head. The inspector pointed towards the door and grinned. "Not a very satisfied customer, it would seem."

"She very rarely is, inspector," Mick O'Reilly said easily. "She's just been complaining about a mark she was given for a piece of work, demanding to know why it wasn't higher." He sighed, pointing to two chairs as an invitation to sit down. "I still can't get my head around it, you know. In my day, if you were given a mark that was lower than what you'd been expecting, you'd immediately feel chastened and think that you had to work harder. But not now. These days, if you get a low mark, then you feel hard done by and automatically think that the piece of work hasn't been marked properly."

The inspector smiled. "It's always got to be someone else's fault!"

"Exactly. That's the culture we live in now." He held up a hand. "Sorry, I probably sound like Victor Meldrew. Most of the students are lovely, I must add. And they're what the job is all about, that's what the taxpayer pays me to do - not the crap to do with pushing paper and attending talking shops listening to over-ambitious idiots trying to sell themselves." He took a sip of his coffee. "But I just can't get my head around this consumer mentality that certain students have."

The inspector thought of his own in-tray and smiled grimly in agreement. "I know what you mean about the paperwork, certainly!" He sat forward in his chair. "Anyway, my colleagues and I have got to find the person who murdered Dr Bumstead. And, of course, that means looking for motives. Have you any idea as to why such a thing has happened?"

Mick O'Reilly and Paul Richardson looked at each other, then Mick replied. "I won't sit here and tell you a load of lies or give you any claptrap, inspector. At the same time, I feel bad about speaking ill of the dead, especially when it's an awful death like this."

"Go on, Dr O'Reilly."

"Well, I do have to say that Delia didn't have many friends."

"Why was that?"

"Well, for a start… oh dear, well, not to make too fine a point of it, she always seemed to get a kick out of stirring up trouble." He turned to his colleague for confirmation.

"That's true," said Paul.

"What sort of trouble?" asked Mark Newport.

"All sorts, mostly concerned with putting colleagues in a bad light," said Mick. "For example, for students in their final year, we have a system of double marking for all major assignments. For example, I'm in the middle of marking essays on poetry appreciation now. So Paul will run his eyes over them, and if we disagree about a mark, we normally compromise and suggest a mark somewhere in between. The external examiner sees the scripts as well, so there's hardly any chance of a student being badly done to. It's normal practice everywhere."

"So what was the problem whenever Dr Bumstead was involved in the marking?"

"Well, she nearly always gave lower marks – she nearly always marked any stuff down."

"But you'd discuss this with her?"

Mick O'Reilly laughed. It was a bitter, cynical laugh that somehow carried with it memories of past problems. "With respect to the dead, you couldn't discuss anything with Delia, inspector. She was always right."

"And it wasn't just that," said Paul. "She'd then go off to management and start spreading it around that the section didn't have high academic standards."

"Exactly," said Mick. "But she didn't give a damn about academic standards really. All she wanted to do was cause trouble for people, usually by making herself look big and others look small."

"You have another colleague in the English section, haven't you?" said Ray Farrar. "A part-timer, I believe."

Mick O'Reilly nodded. "That's right, Frances – Frances McAteer. She just does six hours a week for us. She's very good, as well. It's a pity she can't be full-time."

"I assume there aren't enough hours for her to go full-time?" The inspector said the words casually, not too sure himself where this part of the conversation was going, but anxious to find out as much as possible about the staff, particularly those in the section that Delia Bumstead had belonged to.

He was interested to see that the two lecturers exchanged sad, knowing smiles. "Well, there's a bit of history there, too, inspector."

"Go on, Dr O'Reilly."

"Well, Frances could have gone full time if one of her specialist options had been accepted on the degree. But Delia, ever anxious to appear the good girl in the eyes of upper management, sent an email to everyone arguing that we couldn't afford another full-time member of staff, and that the option wasn't academically viable – to use her words – anyway."

"So what happened?"

"A message came from on high, from the Assistant Director for Resources, praising what Delia had said, saying that this was an excellent example of a member of staff being aware of the need for cost-cutting. Efficiency gains, I think the phrase is – what it means is that people have to take on more and more jobs for no extra pay. Anyway, I went crazy, and told Delia what I thought of her."

"What did she say?"

"She said that this amounted to harassment, and that she'd get the union onto it. It blew over in the end – but it meant that poor Frances couldn't get full-time work, or get her option onto the syllabus."

"I see," said the inspector thoughtfully. "And was she like this with other colleagues in the department, or just with her immediate colleagues in the English section?"

"Oh, she was the same with everyone. She didn't try it on with Terry Trotter so much – he's head of the French section – because he'd give back as good as he got. Don't get me wrong, Terry's a good bloke, even though he sometimes rubs people up the wrong way."

"Did she have any friends on the staff?"

"Only Liz Goodwin. She's a part-timer in the French section. She never caused trouble for her – in fact, she always supported her on things."

"But how was she able to cause trouble with colleagues from other sections?" asked Mark Newport.

"Well, she'd go around asking the students how so-and-so taught, if so-and-so started lectures on time, and so on. Then she'd spread rumours and gossip about them. She used to make life hell on earth for Jim Gregory, who left at Christmas to look after his wife, who's terminally ill."

"She was also in charge of student questionnaires," said Paul. "Every year, students are asked to comment on how subjects have been taught, how much written work has been given out, that sort of thing. So she'd change some of the answers, or throw away positive comments on staff, to make the overall impression negative."

"But why was she allowed to get away with all this?" asked the inspector.

Mick O'Reilly leaned forward in his chair. "Because there's no leadership in the department, inspector. Also, Delia made sure she made friends in high places." He sighed and shook his head. "At the same time..."

"Yes, please go on, Dr O'Reilly."

"Well, I know she was a pain in the arse – and that's putting it mildly – but, in a way, I actually felt sorry for her at times... I mean, she must have been dreadfully unhappy, mustn't she? As Frances McAteer once said about her, if all you want to do is make others unhappy, you must be unhappy yourself, mustn't you?"

The inspector looked at the man and slowly nodded in agreement. "I agree with you one hundred per cent, Dr O'Reilly." Then a thought struck him as he saw the file in Mark Newport's hand. "By the way, did you ever teach a student called Michael Springer?"

The two lecturers immediately looked at each other. "It's funny you should ask that," said Mick O'Reilly. "Paul mentioned him this morning. Yes, I taught him for a couple of years. He seemed OK, there's nothing special to remember about him, really, though he had a bit of a reputation among the female students, to put it mildly."

"So there's nothing much you can say about him, Dr O'Reilly?"

He sighed and shook his head. "No, not really. He didn't mean all that much to me when he was here – but it was an awful shock to hear about him being murdered. You know, a young person, with their life ahead of them... An awful thing to happen."

"Did you teach him, Mr Richardson?"

"No, he was just before my time. This is my first year here."

"I see. OK, thank you for your help."

As the two policemen got up to leave, the inspector noticed a team photograph of Tranmere Rovers pinned to the wall.

"Do you manage to see them?" he asked, smiling and pointing to the photograph.

"A few times a year, when we go to see relatives. My wife's family's from that area, as well. I take my sons to see them if there's a home game on." Mick O'Reilly gestured towards Paul. "And this fellow supports Lincoln City."

Paul gave an embarrassed grin, as though something questionable about his character had been uncovered.

"Right," said Ray Farrar. "Well, I'm a Rochdale fan, and my colleague confesses to following Grimsby Town."

Mick O'Reilly grinned. "So we're all masochists, then?"

"Some of us more than others," said Ray Farrar. "I also run a junior football team."

Chapter 5

"Can you tell us where you were this morning before coming into the College, Dr Carruthers?"

"Do I have to answer that question?"

Detective Sergeant Gillian Taylor crossed her legs, picked a long blond hair from her black trousers and gave him an alluring smile. "Yes, Dr Carruthers."

"And what happens if I don't?"

Her smile became even more attractive. "Then I'll have you arrested for obstructing the police in the course of their enquiries into a murder."

"Also, Dr Carruthers, any attempt to hinder our enquiries could well be construed as a desire on your part to hide something material to the case." Detective Constable Alan Henry leaned forward in his leather jacket, his dark eyes fixed on the man.

The man sneered. "Oh, I see. Typical of the police. Blackmail, eh? If I don't kow-tow and co-operate then things will be made difficult for me."

"Dr Carruthers," said Gillian Taylor in a tone that would be used when reproving a naughty child, "we aren't here to play games. We are here to try and find out who murdered one of your colleagues. Now would you please answer the question?"

She tried to ignore the dull headache that this troublesome man was making even worse. *I've got to cut down. Why did I have that vodka on top of all that wine last night? I drank loads on Saturday night, as well...*

Carruthers looked at her and then at the floor. "I had arranged to see someone." He said the words in an almost childlike sulk.

"Can we have this person's name and address, Dr Carruthers?"

"What for?" He stared at her, his face tilting upwards in an almost imperious pose.

She tried not to sigh. "To corroborate your story, Dr Carruthers." She cocked her head to one side. "Look, your private life is no concern of ours, Dr Carruthers. Everything will be done with the greatest confidentiality and discretion, I assure you."

"Her name is Valerie Salter." He reached across to a writing pad on the other side of his desk and scribbled down the name. "I haven't a clue where she's living or what she's doing."

The lecturer had suddenly lost a lot of his earlier bravado and assertiveness, which immediately interested the two police officers.

"Who is this Valerie Salter, Dr Carruthers?"

His fingers lightly drummed his desk. "She's a former student."

"I see."

"No, you don't see."

"I don't see what?"

"It isn't like that, it isn't what you're thinking."

"And what would I be thinking, Dr Carruthers?"

"The obvious, shall we say. That I'm having a relationship with her. Well, I'm not. Sorry to disappoint you. I haven't laid eyes on the girl or heard from her since the day she graduated."

The policewoman smiled. "Dr Carruthers, the thought didn't cross my mind. As I've already said, we aren't interested in any relationships you might or might not have with former students."

"Well, whether you are or you aren't, Valerie will be able to put you right on that score. She was one of my personal tutees when she was here, and that was all."

"So may I ask you why you arranged to see her, Dr Carruthers?"

"Because she phoned me and asked me if she could see me and ask me about something. And before you ask, I've no idea what it was about. She seemed anxious about it, whatever it was."

"In what way did she seem anxious?"

He shrugged his shoulders. "The tone of her voice. She seemed jittery, a bit stressed. I said that she could see me here, but she didn't seem to want to do that. So I suggested a café bar in town, the *Bar Italiano*. I went there this morning and waited for what must have been half an hour, but she didn't come. I've no idea why. And if you don't believe me, you can check with the bar – there are witnesses who will be able to tell you I was there from nine o'clock to about half past."

"And do you have a contact number for Valerie Salter, Dr Carruthers?"

He shook his head. "No, I don't. I don't know where she is, I have no idea how she can be contacted. When she phoned me, it was from a public phone box."

Without knowing why, Detective Sergeant Gillian Taylor was intrigued. "Thank you, Dr Carruthers."

Frances McAteer was a fair-haired woman in her mid-thirties with candid blue eyes and a permanent half smile which suggested that she found life to be something of a tiresome joke. Ray Farrar noticed that, according to her file, she had been a part-timer at the College for six years.

Given the history of antagonism involving her failure to secure a full-time post, the inspector wanted to explore this area.

"Mrs McAteer," he said, noticing the wedding ring, "can you tell us how you got on with Dr Bumstead."

"I didn't, inspector. And I would be lying to say otherwise."

"I see. Why was that?"

"Because she seemed to enjoy being nasty to people." She put a hand to her mouth. "I know it's wrong to speak ill of the dead..."

"No, no, it's all right, Mrs McAteer. We appreciate your truthfulness." The inspector leaned forward in his chair. "I understand that you've been wanting to obtain a full-time post here."

"She smiled. Yes, well, that was true at the time. I'd been promised a full-time post, but it didn't work out, thanks to Delia telling the powers-that-be that the College couldn't afford it. I think Mick was more upset than I was about it. I know he appears the brash comedian, but he's very sensitive really, and worried about other people's feelings. He'd only just become head of section, so felt that Delia had got her own way through his inexperience at this sort of thing. But it wasn't his fault. You could never be prepared for anything where Delia was concerned. I think she spent her life plotting."

"I see. But now," he said, smiling and holding both hands up defensively, "and please don't take this the wrong way, but I suppose there must be a chance for you to get full-time employment here, given what's happened."

She laughed in a relaxed way. "Don't worry, inspector, I didn't bump her off to get her job." She suddenly gave a flashing smile that transformed her face, somehow making her appear younger. "Last week, I found out that I'm pregnant, after ten years of trying."

Ray Farrar smiled and sat back in his chair. "Great news. Congratulations."

"It puts a whole new slant on things, inspector. Looking back, I know I didn't want to be full-time anyway, and Mick has said that he'll re-arrange the timetable around me when the baby's born." Her eyes drifted to the window for a few seconds. "It's a funny way of making a living, you know, higher education."

"In what way, Mrs McAteer?"

"Well, as Mick always says, it can be a bit remote, cut off from everything else, if you allow it to be. I was in school teaching before I came here, and there's quite a different atmosphere. In school teaching, you're teaching kids from all sorts of backgrounds who are there because they have to be. It's more at the coal face, if you like, and that helps to bring about a feeling of unity, of camaraderie, among the staff."

He smiled on hearing something that helped justify his own preconceived ideas about the academic life. "And that doesn't happen in higher education?"

"Not so much, no. It attracts people who tend to be a bit wrapped up in their subject. It attracts very ambitious people, as well. And personal ambition and human warmth aren't exactly natural bedfellows, though I may be wrong."

Some time later, as she was getting up to leave the office, a tear ran down her cheek just as Ray Farrar was shaking hands with her.

"Are you all right, Mrs McAteer?"

She tried to smile, dabbing her cheek. "Yes, thank you. I was just thinking. I suppose it's the news of the baby that's done it. I've been a bit weepy since I got the news. But it's really dawned on me how empty that poor woman's life must have been." She shook her head sadly. "All she could get turned on by was which member of the management lot she could suck up to and which colleague she could make trouble for. God help her."

Rosemary Hepworth sipped her coffee slowly, even though she had inadvertently let it go cold. Although still in shock by the morning's gruesome discovery, she kept thinking of Michael Springer. He'd seemed a nice enough lad, she thought, a bit sure of himself, but always polite and charming. A nice looking young man, always with an eye for the girls. And they always found him attractive in turn. *He even flirted with me whenever he came into the office*, she thought. *Even though I was fifteen years older than him and married. There was that time when he came up to me and put his arm around my waist when I was getting something out of the filing cabinet for him... And his girlfriend came in at that very moment... He really fancied himself with the women... Was that why he had been killed? A jealous boyfriend, perhaps – or even a jealous husband?* She shivered. *A jealous husband...*

She stared into her coffee. Why did the inspector want to have a look at Michael's file? Did he think there could be some link to Delia Bumstead's murder? Surely not. How could that be? Surely not, she thought, swallowing the remaining dregs of her coffee.

No, just one of life's strange coincidences, she told herself, as she switched her attention to the papers littering her desk, deciding which bit of work was to be tackled first.

About half an hour after ending the interview with Frances McAteer, the two policemen were about to end their interview with the look-alike 1950s footballer.

"Well, thank you for your time and your help, Mr Trotter. We'll contact you again if we think of anything or need anything."

"Feel free, anytime you like. I just hope that the culprit's caught." The centre parting glistened in the afternoon sun. "After all, this murder could mean that we're all in danger. There could be someone out there with a grievance against the College in general."

The inspector nodded thoughtfully. "Yes, that isn't an impossibility, of course. But, from what you and other staff have been telling us, Dr Bumstead did often get on the wrong side of people."

The man held out his hands. "Well, this happens in the hurly-burly of college life, inspector. It used to be a lot worse some years ago, believe me."

"Oh?"

"Oh yes. People yelling at each other in staff meetings, people in tears, people running out of staff meetings, people refusing to speak to each other for ages..." The man sat back and stared at the wall, the mist of nostalgia in his eyes. "Oh, yes, they were the days, there was some blood-letting then, I'm telling you. It's all a bit humdrum now."

"A bit boring?"

"Yes, exactly."

"I see. And did you and Dr Bumstead ever have arguments, harsh words?"

"Well, we had disagreements now and then." The centre parting suddenly leaned forward in the chair. "But it was all purely professional, inspector. There was never anything personal in it, never anything malicious."

"OK, thank you, Mr Trotter. We'll contact you again, should the need arise." Ray Farrar moved to get from his chair, when he suddenly raised a finger. "Oh, there's one other thing."

"Yes?"

"Well, you mentioned before the possibility of there being someone with a grudge against the staff."

The man pulled a face. "Well, yes…"

"Do you think that this could extend to students here, as well?" At the man's apparent puzzlement, he went on. "I'm referring to the recent murder of one of your former students."

"Ah, Michael Springer, poor lad. Oh, I see what you mean." He narrowed his eyes. "It's a bit far from here to Manchester, though, isn't it? Surely Michael's murder and Delia's aren't linked in some way?"

"No, I'm sure you're right, Mr Trotter. I believe he had an eye for the women, though."

Trotter gave a little laugh of sadness. "Well, haven't they all! Yes, I suppose he did, really. He certainly had plenty of girlfriends. He did have a reputation for being a real charmer with the women!"

A minute or two later, Terry Trotter opened the door to find a nervous-looking man with short dark hair and faintly tinted glasses standing there.

"Hello, Jean-Luc. So you're next."

"Yes. I am shitting the trousers."

"Well, there's no need to." Terry Trotter playfully punched him on the arm, almost knocking him sideways. "After all, Jean-Luc, it wasn't you who did it, was it?"

The man pointed at himself, terror in his eyes. "Me? Non, non! I never liked

44

the woman, there were times I wanted to knock off her block – but kill her?"

"Only joking, Jean-Luc!"

The Belgian came into the room and nervously shook hands with the two policemen. He sat down before being asked, trying to avoid eye contact.

"Mr Lafarge, can you please tell us where you were this morning?"

"Ah, yes. I was stuck on the motorway. I had trouble with the car, the engine, the man said." He dabbed at his forehead with a paper tissue. "Two weeks running, you know. Last week, I had a blow job in the High Street."

"I beg your pardon?"

"One of the tyres – I had a blow job with one of the tyres." He made a vague movement with his hand.

"Oh, a tyre blew, I see…"

"That car has something wrong all the time. The mechanic came and explained, but I have forgotten what he said."

"And that was all you did this morning?"

The man's eyes immediately looked fearful. "Well, I had to phone someone."

"I see. Who?"

"The mother of a girl I teach French to, to tell her I can't come to their house this week." His eyes suddenly became beseeching. "I haven't told the tax people – but I promise I will! Everyone does it!"

The inspector smiled. "Mr Lafarge, please calm yourself. Compared to a murder, I think your tax situation is not terribly important."

The man rubbed the palms of his hands on the tissue. "Yes, I see. So you won't report me?"

"No, Mr Lafarge." The inspector changed his sitting position. "Tell me, how did you get on with Dr Bumstead?"

"I did not get on with her! Nobody did! It was impossible to, she was always stirring the shit!"

"I see. In what way?"

"Criticising people, causing trouble! You'd come into work, scared of what was in your pigeon-hole!"

"Things in your pigeon-hole? Such as?"

"Notes from students, complaining about your class, complaining about the way you marked their work – and they were always her favourites! I always remember how difficult she made things for Susan, who teaches Geography, and all because of Bobby."

"Pardon? Who's Bobby?"

"Susan's dog. Susan Barrow, who teaches Geography. She often brings him into work with her."

"She brings her dog into the College?"

"Yes, she takes him for walks around the campus when she hasn't got a class. Anyway, one day, Bobby did a wee right outside Delia's office. When Delia came out, she stepped on it and went arse over bum."

"Was she hurt?"

"A little. Terry Trotter and I saw it. It was the only time I ever saw Terry Trotter laugh."

"So there were frequent arguments between Dr Bumstead and other staff, then, Mr Lafarge?"

"All the time! At meetings, especially! Shouting off her mouth! Always throwing a sponge in the works!"

Mark Newport caught the man's eye. "But surely, Mr Lafarge," he said, thinking of what Terry Trotter had said, "these were just disagreements about policy, that can happen in any workplace? Surely there was nothing personal about them?"

"They were always personal! If anyone says otherwise, they are lying through their tooth!" The man, while relieved that his tax misdemeanours had been forgotten about, wanted nevertheless to be seen to be helpful and so became very talkative. "She thought she was perfect!" He tapped his nose. "But she wasn't!"

The inspector found this remark interesting, though he couldn't explain to himself why. "In what way wasn't she perfect, Mr Lafarge?"

"Well, she always made comments about staff being ill, saying *she* was never ill. She always accused me of swinging the iron. But," he wagged a finger and half turned his head, smiling knowingly, "she was off ill for a week about three years ago. She was supposed to have flu. But I saw her in town, looking into a shop window." He looked at each of them in turn, suddenly confident, inviting a response.

"Do go on, Mr Lafarge, this is most helpful."

"Good. And you know what she was doing?"

46

"What was she doing, Mr Lafarge?"

"She was crying." He sat back in his chair, the earnest eyes swivelling from one policeman to the other. "Oh yes, wetting herself crying. Then when she came back to work, she asked if she could change the tutorial group she had, and swapped with someone else."

"Did you find out why she wanted to change the group for another?"

"No. I just thought it was strange. Especially from her, because she never seemed to let anything get at her. The more stress or aggro there was, the more she enjoyed it. Crazy!"

"Was Dr O'Reilly the Head of English then?"

"No, but he was here. The Head of English retired, then the poor sod dropped dead a week later! I was so shocked, you could have knocked me down with a sledgehammer!"

When the conversation started to peter out, the inspector looked at his watch, then glanced at his colleague to see if he had any further questions.

"Fine, Mr Lafarge, thank you for all your help. You have been most helpful, and it's very much appreciated."

The man got up and beamed at them both, preening himself as he did so. "Ah, it is nothing! As long as I have been of help! It is nice to feel appreciated!"

When the Belgian opened the door, Terry Trotter and Dominic Carruthers were talking in the corridor.

"So they haven't arrested you, then, Jean-Luc?" said Dominic Carruthers, with a sideways sneer at the two policemen. "I hope you were careful what you said, knowing you!"

"Hah, you take the piss off me all the time! You all think I know bugger nothing!" He tapped the side of his nose in a knowing gesture. "But you are wrong – I know bugger all!"

Anne Dickinson stood and surveyed the rows of customers in the café where she worked. She was tired, drained, physically and emotionally. The day's events still seemed unreal. Nurse Richmond at the student health centre had advised her to go home and rest. But Anne knew that if she went home, she would be unable to rest. Yes, there was an exam in a couple of weeks' time, and she knew she still had some revision to do – but she also knew that, if she opened a book, she'd be unable to concentrate. Her eyes would be going over the pages mechanically without her brain being able to take anything in. All she would see in front of her would be, not the printed pages, but the staring eyes and bloodstained head of the person who had been one of her English lecturers.

Suddenly, she was aware of her friend's face staring at her from the other side of the counter. Nurse Richmond was with her.

"It's all right, Anne," said the nurse, her kindly red face grinning. "Geraldine hasn't brought me here to check up on you! We just met by chance in the street."

Anne smiled. "I'll believe you. Would you like a cup of tea?" She lowered her voice. "On the house?"

"Certainly not on the house, Anne," said the nurse, her grin going even wider. "Go on, we'll have one." She turned to Geraldine as a sign that she was paying for them both.

"Are you all right, Anne?" said Geraldine. "You looked miles away. You shouldn't be here, you know, you should be back at the flat."

She shook her head. "No, I'm OK, Geraldine. If I go back to the flat I'll only mope. Besides, like I said this morning, I need the money. I'm in debt enough already. If I apply to extend my loan, my parents'll go mad with worry. They think I'm going to be in debt for the rest of my life as it is. I just can't afford not to work."

"OK. As long as you're sure you're all right…"

"Yeah, I'm fine. I'm only on here until half eight – I'll be back before nine, then we can have a few drinks. Claire and Paula are coming round, as well, aren't they? Maybe we could get a take-away."

Anne had to take an order from a couple who had just come in, leaving Geraldine and nurse Richmond chatting. Then she went to a small area which stretched a little behind the till area to clear a few tables. She was carrying a pile of plates towards the kitchen area when a young woman with jet black hair who had been sitting near one of the front windows, morosely sipping a large mug of coffee, suddenly got up and left the table. Without saying a word, she indicated to Anne that she had left the payment for the coffee next to the till. Nurse Richmond's eyes followed her as she went out of the café.

"Good heavens, fancy seeing her here…I thought she'd gone back to

London… Has she got a job here, I wonder…"

"Who, nurse Richmond?" said Anne.

"The young woman who just went out."

"Was she a student at the College?" asked Geraldine.

"Yes, she was… Yes, a few years ago." Nurse Richmond suddenly appeared nervous, preoccupied.

"I thought she must have been," said Geraldine. "I noticed her on the campus a few times today. She was sitting in the union coffee bar for ages on her own.".

The nurse suddenly smiled. "Oh, was she? Yes, she's one of our old students, she got her degree a couple of years ago. A nice young woman… Just a year before your time, Geraldine. She must have left the year you started." She nodded her head slowly. "Valerie Salter… I had no idea she was back here. Perhaps I should have spoken to her…"

"Your coffee, nurse Richmond. You looked miles away then!"

The woman abruptly came back to the present. "Er, yes, thank you, Anne…"

Chapter 6

They were about to interview Liz Goodwin in the same room where they had spoken to Frances McAteer, a small study set aside exclusively for part-time staff, when Ray Farrar's mobile rang. The familiar voice of Bill Foster, the police pathologist, spoke into his ear.

"Oh, hi, Bill. Thanks for getting back to us. Anything interesting?"

"Well, nothing much besides the obvious, Ray. Death occurred at, let's see now, oh, between eight and half eight this morning. The weapon was a heavy instrument, possibly a hammer from the look of the injuries. Three blows to the head."

"Three? God, they meant business, then."

"Yes, they certainly did. A frenzied attack. There must have been a lot of blood flying around."

"So anyone doing it would have needed a change of clothing?"

"Well, unless they were very careful about not being very near her when they hit her, yes."

"No other tell-tale signs you can give us?"

"Nothing at the moment, Ray. There are fingerprints on the door-knob, according to forensics, but I assume they'll be off the student who went into her room, or off the cleaners. Has the family been informed?"

"Well, we've been trying to contact her husband, Bill. He's away on business somewhere, we believe."

"And how about the children?"

"No, she hasn't got any. It says so on her personal file. Hold on, I'll just double check" The inspector re-examined the file in front of him. "No, no kids. Married, but no children."

"Then the file's a bit out of date, Ray."

"What?"

"Well, we've been working on her, as you can imagine. And she's given birth at some time or other. There's no doubt about that."

"Are you sure?"

"Oh yes."

He rubbed his chin. "Sorry, Bill, I wasn't doubting your judgement for one moment. It's just that her file says she didn't have any."

"No, there's no doubt about it, Ray. She's definitely given birth."

"OK… Right, Bill, thanks." The phone was suddenly slippery in his sweaty hand.

"She might have had a child, of course, and lost it, through illness or whatever. It can happen."

"Yes, that's true, I suppose."

There was a silence of about five seconds. "You don't sound too convinced, Ray."

"Well, you know me, Bill, I'm never convinced about anything. Anyway, thanks for ringing. Get back to me if you come across anything else."

"OK. By the way, a good game yesterday – I thought the kids played well. Who have we got next week?"

"Creek End, away."

"Ah, a tough one – and they have noisy parents! Anyway, Ray, I'll be in touch if anything else crops up."

"So it's this woman called Liz Goodwin next, Mark."

"What she's got to say should be interesting, sir, given that she seems to be the only person here who had any time for Delia Bumstead."

"Yes… Anyway, let's bring her in." He looked at his watch. "We've got to see the people from the History section yet, then the Head and Assistant Head."

Ray Farrar opened the door to find that Liz Goodwin had not yet come. He took advantage of the break by going to the toilet. On his way down the corridor, he noticed that Dominic Carruthers and the young woman with frizzy hair who had applauded his intervention at the meeting in the lecture theatre were talking earnestly in a classroom. On his way back from the toilet he called in to where Gillian Taylor and Alan Henry were.

"I assume you sorted out the mad revolutionary, Gillian?"

She laughed, then peered at her notes. "One interesting bit that Alan and I got out of him, sir."

"Go on."

"Well, he seemed unwilling to say where he was this morning before coming here, but finally he told us that he'd arranged to see a former student. When we asked him what it was about, he said that he didn't know himself, that she'd contacted him because she wanted to talk to him about something. Then he said he didn't see her in the end because she didn't turn up. He has witnesses, or so he claims." She pulled a face as though displeased with herself. "I just don't know, sir, I can't explain it, but there's something fishy about it. At the same time, I think he's telling the truth. I hope I'm making sense. Alan got the same impression, as well."

"Did you get the student's name?"

"Yes, someone called Valerie Salter. He said she finished here the year before last, and that this was the first time she'd been in touch with him since she left."

"Right, might be interesting, you never know. OK, well done, we can soon follow that up. Anyway, you've got his little supporter next, haven't you, from the Sociology section. The stroppy-looking one with the frizzy hair. What's her name again?"

"Lucinda Hobbs-Smithers."

He threw back his head and laughed. "And she was applauding her colleague's attack on the class system! A very working class name!" He was about to close the door when he remembered something. "You've got a woman called Veronica Makepeace later, as well. Mark and I saw her have quite an emotional argument with a woman called Harriet Bond from the History section. She could be interesting."

He returned to the interviewing room just as Mark was opening the door for a small, thin woman with mousy hair tied at the back with a pink ribbon.

"Liz Goodwin?"

The woman nodded as she took a seat, giving each of them a very brief handshake. She had wide blue eyes which restlessly stared at them and at everything in the room, while her head and body somehow remained still. Her hands were on her lap, tightly joined.

"Miss Goodwin, could you please tell us how you got on with Dr Bumstead?"

Her voice was quiet but assertive. "I got on fine with her."

"Really? All the time?"

The large eyes stared at him, unblinking, then swivelled to Mark Newport and back again. "Yes. All the time."

"There are staff, several staff, who say that she could be difficult to get on with, Miss Goodwin. I take it that you don't agree with them?"

"She had her faults, haven't we all? But she was also kind and supportive to me."

"In what way?"

The woman swallowed before replying, both policemen noted. "Professionally, socially, various ways."

"You're a part-time member of staff, Miss Goodwin. Would I be right in thinking that you'd very much like to be full-time?"

"Yes, that's true. And Delia was the first person, the only person really, who went out of her way to help me." A look of contempt briefly clouded her face. "More than the Head of Department or the Assistant Head of Department could be bothered to do, it has to be said."

"I see. And did Dr Bumstead support the other part-timers in their wish to get full-time status?"

"I have no idea, inspector."

"You see, we get the distinct impression that she didn't, Miss Goodwin. In fact, it would seem that you were the only person on the staff that she got on with. It also seems that you were the only person on the staff who, not to put too fine a point on it, didn't cross swords with her. Mutual support, if you like."

"Yes, it was a case of mutual support, I suppose."

When he saw the still hands suddenly fidget, he knew it was time to probe further. "Was the mutual support purely in the professional domain, Miss Goodwin, or did it stretch to life in general?"

The eyes looked down to her hands for several seconds. When she raised them, they were brimming with tears. She swallowed again and put a shaking hand to her mouth. She made a conscious effort to control herself, then started to speak, very slowly.

"Two years ago, I had an abortion." The large eyes examined each policeman in turn. "Nobody here knew about it. Nobody still does."

"Don't worry, Miss Goodwin, you have our word that this is all highly confidential-"

She waved a hand to interrupt him. A tear was running down her cheek. "The father... well, he said he didn't want to know. He told me to get rid of it, to use

53

his words. He said that, if I didn't, he'd stop our relationship. So I got rid of it – and he finished with me anyway." She slowly shook her head repeatedly. "I got rid of my child. I still can't believe what I did." Her voice was barely audible.

Her face suddenly became contorted with grief. Her body shook. She raised her eyes to the ceiling as though asking God for forgiveness. She accepted a tissue that Mark Newport handed her, blew her nose, then slowly composed herself, her cheeks streaked with dried tears.

"It's all right, Miss Goodwin. Go on whenever you're ready…"

"One day, Delia called in here to see me about something, and saw me like this. She asked me what was wrong. I don't know why, I told her everything I've just told you."

A rumble of thunder made Ray Farrar look out of the window, and he saw that the sky was now a mass of threatening grey clouds. It was somehow in keeping with the mood in the room.

"What was her reaction to this, Miss Goodwin?"

She blew her nose before continuing. "Well, I was absolutely flabbergasted."

"Why was that?" He noticed that Mark Newport had also edged forward in his seat.

"Well, she sat down and started crying. I couldn't believe it. It was the first time I had ever seen her show any kind of emotion. And then she told me why she was crying."

"Go on, Miss Goodwin."

"She said that she knew how I felt. She said that she'd lost two children herself."

"Two children?"

"Yes, that's what she said."

"She definitely said *two* children?"

"Yes, two. There's no way I could get anything like that wrong. I said that that was awful, and that I felt for her."

"And did she give you any details, Miss Goodwin?"

"No, and I never asked her for any. We never mentioned the subject again. But, ever since that day, we always supported each other whenever anything arose in the department."

"I see." He slowly turned his pen over in his fingers. "Miss Goodwin, we believe that Dr Bumstead was absent once, through illness. We have reason to think it might have been depression. Did she ever confide in you about it?"

She shook her head. "No, but I remember it quite well. She looked drawn when she came back the following week."

"We also believe that at this time she didn't want to teach a group of students that she had been given, and insisted on changing the group of students for another. Have you any idea why?"

Another shake of the head. "No. Delia could be very private when she wanted to be."

"I'd better warn you from the start, in case you think you can try any of your pushy police methods with me. I've got a degree in Law as well as History."

Gillian Taylor sat back and looked at the woman for a few seconds. It was obvious that Lucinda Hobbs-Smithers was going to attempt to be as awkward as her mentor, Dominic Carruthers. Certainly, her office walls were full of posters proclaiming revolution and overthrow in terms that could never claim to be mild.

"Miss Hobbs-Smithers-"

"Ms."

"I beg your pardon?"

" I'm a *Ms,* not a *Miss.* Can we get that straight, also, if you don't mind?" She smirked as her eyes rested on the policewoman's engagement ring.

Well, you'll certainly never bloody be a Mrs, thought Alan Henry to himself. *And if ever you are, God help the poor sod.*

He missed the next question put by Gillian Taylor because he was busy thinking how interesting it was that those women who most loudly proclaim the feminist cause tend to be the least feminine, that those women who most stridently rant against advances by males tend to be those who would have least cause. He pulled himself up with a start as he realised how such an aggressive and negative reaction to the woman was at odds with the religious and philosophical journey he had been embarked on for the past few months...

What was it about this woman that made him think like this?

He didn't like her the second he had set eyes on her, it was as simple as that, though he didn't know why. And it wasn't through what she was saying. He just didn't like her. Looking at her, he knew that this woman, whatever the cultural or social background she came from, would be a fanatic, quite capable of hurting (or even killing?) anyone who dared to have opinions different to hers, be they political, religious or whatever. *What sort of background, what sort of upbringing, have you had, to turn out like that?* he found himself wondering. *Will you ever be able to come to peace with yourself?*

"How did you get on with Dr Bumstead, Ms Hobbs-Smithers?"

The woman gave a knowing grin. "You mean, did I have a motive for killing her?"

"If you'd just answer the question, please."

She was obviously irked by Gillian Taylor's refusal to get annoyed or raise her voice, and pointedly looked the policewoman up and down before replying.

"Not bad, I suppose. We had the occasional argument over policy, but nothing personal. We only ever exchanged words at meetings. I didn't really know her enough, nor did I particularly want to."

"Why was that, Ms Hobbs-Smithers?"

"Because she was a capitalist."

"A capitalist? In what way?"

"She devoted her life to acquiring the trappings of our hideous and self-seeking society, and didn't want to share her wealth with the dispossessed."

Gillian Taylor looked at the woman for a few seconds before continuing. "I see. Just one more thing, Ms Hobbs-Smithers. What were you doing early this morning?"

"I was in Ford's, the estate agents in the High Street, seeing to the purchase of my second home in the Cotswolds. You can check with them, if you so wish."

The policewoman tried not to give a sad smile. "Thank you, Ms Hobbs-Smithers."

"But you said you would have all the stuff for my stay in France typed out and ready for me to collect! You promised!"

Rosemary Hepworth tried to avoid the student's staring eyes. "Well, yes, I know I did, Robert. But things have been very difficult today, as you may have heard. There's still plenty of time. I'll try to-"

"This just isn't good enough! I'll tell my parents about this! Do you know who my father is?"

An aggressive little loudmouth like you, probably, thought Mick O'Reilly. He caught the secretary's eye from behind the student's back and pulled a face of encouragement and shook his head, telling her not to take any notice.

Rosemary Hepworth was about to say something when the student cut her short.

"Oh, don't bother! I'll be here tomorrow – and if it isn't done then, then my parents will be complaining! You can be sure of that!"

Maureen Threlfall, who was checking something in one of the filing cabinets, turned around and looked at the student, which he took as a sign of encouragement.

"No wonder the department's in the state it's in!" he shouted at the secretary.

Maureen looked at him from over her glasses. "Do you always speak to people like that, Robert?" Her eyes were unblinking.

"It's the only way to get things done! Everyone knows that!"

She slowly closed the drawer of the filing cabinet. "Is that so? Well, Robert, *I* don't speak to people like that." Then she gave him a smile of utter contempt. "But, then again, I'm one of the fifties' children. Not one of Thatcher's."

The aggressive Robert went to say something, but only succeeded in making a noise in his throat and swept out of the office.

"Goodness me," said Rosemary. "The way some people speak to you. Haven't they been taught any manners?"

"On the contrary, Rosemary," said Mick O'Reilly, "people in this country have been taught *not* to have manners. As Maureen's just implied, what do you expect, when we were all told back in the eighties that there's no such thing as society?"

Ray Farrar and Mark Newport were standing at the front door of the building, getting a breath of air, watching the rain slowly soak the grassy surrounds. The air was now fresher, and a patch of blue sky coyly appeared from behind the distant hills. The policemen turned around to go in and continue the interviews, when Ray Farrar spotted Paul Richardson coming out of the office.

"Ah, Mr Richardson, just a quick word, if you don't mind."

"Certainly."

"Your English degree here – is it three or four years?"

"Well, you can do a combination of subjects, but whatever the students choose, all the degrees are three years. They're only four years if the students doing French as a main part of their degree choose to spend a whole year in France, the third year, rather than just a term. Then they come back as fourth-year students to finish their degree."

The inspector bit his lip and nodded his head. "OK, thank you. It's just that, according to her file, Dr Bumstead took four years for her English degree at the University of Cumbria."

Paul Richardson raised a finger. "Yes, that's right, she did. I remember Mick asking her about that a few months ago. She said that she took a year out after the first two years to go around the world."

The policeman nodded. "I see. Thank you."

Seconds later, a Mercedes stopped in front of the building and a tall balding man in an immaculate blue suit and matching tie got out. He left hand gripped a shiny briefcase. Ray Farrar noticed that the man had his eyes glued on him from the moment he left the car, and he knew instinctively who the man was.

"Are you Inspector Farrar?"

"Yes, I am…"

"My name is Barry Bumstead." The eyes were unblinking. "I have just been told that my wife was found murdered this morning."

The tone of voice was detached, factual, though the eyes were intense.

"Yes, I'm afraid that's right, Mr Bumstead. This is my colleague, Detective Sergeant Mark Newport." Ray Farrar noticed that the man didn't even give Mark a glance. "We are terribly sorry, Mr Bumstead. But we do have a few questions to ask. Would you please come this way?"

A minute later, Barry Bumstead was sitting in front of them, his hands joined together, but not tightly, the inspector noticed. In fact, the man seemed to be quite relaxed, given the awfulness of the situation.

"Where did you hear of your wife's death, Mr Bumstead?"

"In Birmingham. I came right away."

"I see. There are certain things, of course, that we have to ask you."

"Yes. Fire ahead." The man sat back in his chair and, seemingly for the first time, glanced at Mark Newport.

"When did you last see your wife?"

"I can't remember."

"You can't remember when you last saw your wife?"

"A week last Friday, I think."

"Mr Bumstead, we believe your wife did her degree at the University of Cumbria. Could you please tell us what her maiden name was?"

"Kennedy. Why do you ask?"

"Because we want to examine every aspect of your wife's past, to see if any links with the present somehow come to light."

His features were still, unchanging. "I see."

Ray Farrar marvelled at the man's demeanour. He had answered the questions as if he had just been asked when he was last in a supermarket. In fact, the more the interview went on, it became horribly clear to both policemen that Barry Bumstead was one of those people – relatively few in number, mercifully – who seem quite devoid of feeling or emotion. His marriage to Delia Bumstead must have been relegated over the years to a legal binding and little else. The inspector thought of people that he and his wife often saw in pubs and restaurants, sitting in total silence with not a single thing to say to each other any more. He felt a terrible sadness, knowing that this must have been like one of those relationships, a marriage as dead as the body he had seen slumped over a desk that morning.

The interview had drawn to a close, and Ray Farrar was opening the office door for the man to leave, when he suddenly turned to him.

"Mr Bumstead, just one more thing. Forgive me for asking this, as it is a very personal question, but did you and Dr Bumstead ever have children?"

The man gave him an inscrutable stare for a few seconds. "No, we didn't. She wasn't able to. Why do you ask?"

Ray Farrar swallowed, his mind racing from what the pathologist had said to what Liz Goodwin had said.

"Because, according to the pathologist, it appears that she did have a child."

For a split second the man's face showed a hint of emotion. "Then the pathologist must be mistaken, inspector."

Maureen Threlfall was still seething at the aggressive Robert's rudeness to her and to Rosemary Hepworth in the office, when she opened the first of three envelopes she had taken from her pigeon hole and read the memo inside it.

To: All Staff

From: Sidney Barker, Marking Assessor

I have noted with some alarm that the profile of marks for student groups does not tally with that prescribed in my memo SB/446XY24, in which I stated that a given group of students should have a set of marks across the performance spectrum. Despite the recommendations in the said memo, there were some groups who, in the December examinations, had marks that were either too high or too low due to the fact that there was more than the normal number of students attaining good, average or poor marks. It is to be hoped that staff do not fall into the same error when marking the summer examinations.

She read the memo again, muttered a mild swear word to herself, then made her way to Mick O'Reilly's office. On the way, she met Frances McAteer.

"Have you got this nonsense, Frances?" she said, waving the sheet.

Frances smiled and nodded. "Yes. Absolutely ridiculous, isn't it?"

Just then Mick came out of his office. "Yes, I know what you're going to say, he said. "A load of rubbish."

"Hasn't Sidney Barker got anything better to do?"

"Well, no, Maureen, simply because churning out mindless nonsense like this is precisely what he gets paid for."

Maureen Threlfall shook her head in frustration. "But what use is it to anyone?"

"It's of use to him, Maureen – it probably gets him forty-odd grand a year, maybe more." Mick suddenly smiled as his eyes swept down the corridor. "Well, speak of the devil."

The two women turned around to see Sidney Barker coming down the corridor towards them. He was a small round man in his early fifties who always walked briskly and who frequently had a clipboard in his hand.

"Sidney, can you please tell us just what this is all about?"

He looked at Mick, his little eyes unblinking. "You know what it's about. It's about the desirability of having an average range of marks for a typical group."

"What do you mean by an average range of marks?"

"Marks which go from quite low to quite high." His voice had risen, both in volume and in pitch. Mick was amused to find that the man's head had also risen, due to the fact that he was practically on tip-toe.

"And what do you mean by a typical group?"

His lips formed a thin line for some seconds before he answered. "Students who should obtain the said range of marks."

Mick grinned down at him. "But what if there is an exceptionally high number of good students in the group? Or an exceptionally high number of scivers? Or if there's an excessively high number of fair-to-middling students?"

"Just what are you trying to say?"

"What I'm trying to say, Sidney, is that there is no such thing as a typical group. Just like there is no such thing as a typical person. They're all different."

"Each group is going to have to reflect a range of marks from top to bottom, and that's all there is to it!"

The man was shouting by now, his voice so high-pitched that Mick was wondering that if it went any higher the man would end up being heard only by dogs.

"And that's all there is to it, Sidney? So groups aren't composed of individuals, then?" Frances McAteer was trying not to laugh.

"My memo SB/446XY24 says it all. It is to be read and followed. All Colleges do this sort of thing now. It's a necessary mechanism, a valuable watchdog. Last year's directive 7274HTW states that categorically."

"Sidney," said Maureen Threlfall quietly. "Do you ever get excited or moved when you hear Handel's *Messiah* or *If I Were A Carpenter* by The Four Tops or *Hello Goodbye* by David Grey?"

"*Spirit In The Sky* by Norman Greenbaum is the one for me," said Mick O'Reilly with a smile that was mischievous yet serious. "A cry of faith, of belief – pure theology."

"Aren't there times, Sidney," said Maureen, "when your spirit rises, when your senses become acute, and you have indefinable feelings of joy when you see a fantastic goal being scored, or indescribable feelings of pain when you see a picture of a child in Angola with no roof over its head?"

"I don't know what you're talking about," he said.

She laid a sympathetic hand on his sleeve. "I know you don't, Sidney."

Chapter 7

After a brief but animated discussion about their conversation with Barry Bumstead, the two policemen knocked on the door of Maureen Threlfall's office and, at her call, went in to find she was already pouring out tea and coffee for them. Ray Farrar noticed with some satisfaction that there was also a plate of custard creams on the desk.

"Right, Mrs Threlfall, as you can imagine, there are a couple of things we've got to ask. First of all, can you tell us where you were between eight and half eight this morning?"

"Yes, I was on my way here. I suppose I must have got here at about half past eight, that's the time I normally arrive. It depends on the traffic on the main road, of course. If the traffic's bad, then I sometimes don't get in until about twenty to nine."

"Fine, thank you. Tell me, how did you get on with Dr Bumstead?"

"With great difficulty," she said with a wistful smile. "Sorry, I know that sounds a clever answer, but she did make life very difficult for people. She was always one for poking her nose into things, into matters that were the business of other sections and not just her own section. It sounds terrible, I know…"

Ray Farrar held his hand over his mouth as he ate one of the custard creams. "No, please go on, Mrs Threlfall."

"Well, and this is no exaggeration, she seemed to thrive on conflict. I know that sounds over the top, but I'm afraid it's true – in my opinion, anyway. She would pick arguments with people for the sake of it. And she was always checking up on people, bringing things up in staff meetings, to see if people had remembered to do things that were their responsibility. And if they hadn't, she'd be nasty with them, and then divulge it to management."

"Did you ever have disagreements with her?"

The woman nodded. "Nearly all the time. It was as though she hated to leave you in peace. Probably because she was never at peace with herself. She seemed to be consumed by a restless, nervous energy. I could never imagine her sitting at home watching the telly or reading a newspaper. She lived and breathed this place." Her eyes were suddenly thoughtful and she gave a tiny involuntary laugh.

"What is it, Mrs Threlfall?"

"Well, I always remember coming back, it must be a couple of years ago now, in January after the Christmas break. I went to my pigeon hole, and, as ever, there was a note from Delia reminding me about something – I can't remember what, but something minor, petty, if you like. And she had written the date on the note. And the date was 31 December." She shook her head and sighed.

"Do go on, Mrs Threlfall."

"Well, I sat there looking at the date, and I immediately felt a terrible sadness for her. Doesn't that sound smug?"

"No, not at all."

"You see, every New Year, my husband and I see our friends from Teesside, either at their place or ours – we haven't missed for over thirty years. And I thought, looking at Delia's note, that while I was in Teesside, relaxing and enjoying myself, filling myself with food and drink, poor Delia had had nothing better to do, on New Year's Eve, than to write a note to do with this place. And do you know what the saddest thing about it was?"

"What, Mrs Threlfall?"

"The saddest thing about it all was that she'll have written the date on that note on purpose, to show me how hardworking she was. Pathetic." She suddenly reached across and passed the plate of biscuits. "Do have some more."

"Thank you," they said in unison.

"Sorry about that diatribe, by the way. But that was Delia summed up – you were driven mad by her, yet at the same time you knew deep down that you felt awfully sorry for her."

"Can you tell us anything about her home life, Mrs Threlfall?"

"Oh dear, well… from what I can gather, I think it was pretty well non-existent. Her husband was away on business more than he was at home, I think. I only saw him once. He came to a Christmas do for staff and partners, sat next to my husband, and made no attempt at conversation all evening. It wasn't shyness as such, it was more like a show of impersonal superiority, if you know what I mean. He just sat there looking around at everyone as if we were interesting specimens in a zoo." She suddenly giggled. "Mind you, Mick O'Reilly would say that that's what some people in this place are! Aren't I awful!"

Ray Farrar suppressed a smile. "And how did she get on with the students,

Mrs Threlfall?"

"I'm not too sure – though she always knew how *you* got on with *your* students!"

"In what way?"

"Well, she made it her business to know, snooping, asking questions about other people's teaching, that sort of thing."

"We understand that a couple of years ago there was one particular group of students that she didn't want to teach."

She sat still and quiet for a few seconds as she finished a biscuit, her mind clearly focused on the past. "Yes, that's right. Now, let me see… Yes, there was a tutorial group that she'd been given, then she suddenly asked Mick if she could swap with him the one that he was to teach. I remember Mick mentioning it, saying how surprised he was by the request. In fact, she was insistent on it, she practically refused to teach the group." She gave a little laugh. "Mind you, Delia was always insistent on everything!"

"And the swap went ahead?"

"Yes, Mick changed it for her – and for some peace!" She played with the spoon in her saucer. "They were a nice group, too, that Mick ended up with – I remember one of them, especially, as I taught him History." A sigh followed. "The poor lad."

Ray Farrar brought the second half of his custard cream away from his lips. "Who, Mrs Threlfall?"

"It's terrible, really. One of the students in the group that Delia refused to teach was found murdered just recently. Michael Springer, his name was. Fancied himself, but a nice lad deep down. They still haven't found out who did it, have they?"

The two policemen tried not to look at each other. "No, I believe enquiries are still proceeding. And Dr Bumstead had given no reason as to why she wanted to swap groups?"

"None at all. But there was no way she was going to teach this particular group. And if ever Delia dug her heels in about something, then that was that, there was no shifting her."

"Does the department keep records of all the various groups, Mrs Threlfall?" asked Mark Newport.

65

"Not of all the various option groups and such like, no, I wouldn't have thought so." She suddenly clicked her fingers. "But maybe I can help you, if that's what you want."

"Well, it might be helpful for our enquiries, Mrs Threlfall," said Ray Farrar.

"All the students in this particular group did History or French as well as English, so I'll have kept a copy of all the names." She grinned. "I'm a terrible hoarder – ask my husband!"

She opened a small filing cabinet and thumbed through it for a minute or two, then produced a thin folder. "Here we are – ah, I've even got spare copies, so you can have one each!"

Ray Farrar took his copy, smiling up at her. "That might be most helpful, Mrs Threlfall." He felt excited, on edge, though he didn't know why, as he allowed her to top up his coffee and tempt him with yet another custard cream.

"You're being totally unreasonable!"

Terry Trotter pushed out his chest and looked her straight in the face. "And what is unreasonable about being expected to do what you're paid to do, Lucinda?"

She ran her hands through her frizzy hair. "How can you expect me to produce a new mark sheet by tomorrow? I can't do it, Rosemary will have to do it."

The secretary tried to make herself small behind her PC. "Er, well I'll do my best, but I've got such a lot on…"

"Exactly!" he snapped. "Rosemary's snowed under with work as it is." He lowered his voice. "Lucinda, it will take all of twenty minutes. What's so awful about that?" He wagged a knowing finger. "And don't forget, part of it is your own fault – if you hadn't got those averages wrong, more than half of the marks would have been all right anyway."

Lucinda Hobbs-Smithers stamped her foot. "You've always got to have the last bloody word, haven't you?"

"Lucinda, with people like you, I feel I've always got to."

She flung a pile of files onto the office counter, making Rosemary Hepworth jump. "Oh piss off, you're just as bad as that lot."

"What lot, Lucinda?"

"Those fascist pigs whose ridiculous questions I've had to answer! You should be with them! The establishment's lackeys!"

He openly laughed at her. "Lucinda, you're being silly."

"And you're being a pig! No bloody wonder Delia didn't want to share that group with you!"

"Which group? What are you talking about?"

"The group that she didn't want to teach a few years ago!"

"Don't talk nonsense! We teach two different academic subjects, for God's sake. Her not wanting to teach that group had nothing to do with me – I've no idea why she didn't want to teach them."

Lucinda picked up the files that she had thrown onto the counter and stormed out of the office.

"Oh dear," said Rosemary quietly, when she was sure she was out of earshot. "She is a rather complicated person, isn't she?"

Terry Trotter picked an envelope out of his pigeon hole. "No, actually, Rosemary. Lucinda isn't complicated at all."

"Oh, er, what do you mean, exactly?"

"Lucinda isn't complicated at all, Rosemary. In fact, Lucinda is very easy to analyse. Quite simply, she's the most important person in the world. She's one of those people who, from the day she was born, has been told by mummy and daddy that she's extra special, and has grown up convinced of the fact. She doesn't believe in putting herself out for anybody except Lucinda Hobbs-Smithers."

As he, too, left the office, Gillian Taylor smiled to herself in the corridor, thinking that a lot of what she had overheard was most interesting. Her hangover had gone, as well.

Harriet Bond was Maureen Threlfall's colleague in the History section. Besides their physical differences, Ray Farrar realised within a matter of seconds that the two women couldn't be more unlike. Harriet Bond, thought the policeman as he looked at her, was one of those people who don't just come into a room, they make an entrance. Whereas Maureen Threlfall seemed quite unable to take herself seriously, this woman was continually on her dignity. She also had a tendency, whether through a desire to make others feel uncomfortable or through an unconscious habit, of peering at people from above the top of her glasses, her wide lips set in a determined line. Ray Farrar put her to be in her early to mid forties.

"How long have you been on the staff here, Miss Bond?"

"This will be my fourth full year." The voice was clipped and measured, quiet but assured. Looking at her formal posture, Ray Farrar guessed that she had received the benefits of a private education and speech lessons.

"And how did you get on with Dr Bumstead, Miss Bond?"

"Not terribly well, shall we say. She was one of those people who are absolutely full of themselves, who talk at you rather than to you." The stare came over the glasses. "Do you understand?"

"Absolutely, Miss Bond," said Ray Farrar with one of his most charming smiles. "So I take it you didn't meet socially, then?"

The woman gave a superior titter, then shook her head. "Oh my, no, no. I'm afraid my social life has wider horizons than that, Mr Farrar. Oh, good heavens, no. Dr Bumstead's social life, if indeed she had one worthy of the name, restricted itself to dinner parties and Sunday lunches with the College's management clique." A long thin hand brushed a hair from her black skirt. "Delia always knew on which side her bread was buttered."

"How do staff normally get on with each other, Miss Bond?"

"Well, you try and do your own thing while being as pleasant as possible to others, just like in most walks of life, I suppose. I don't go out of my way to be with people I feel I have very little in common with, that would make life more taxing than it is already. But I do try to be civil."

"Of course." He knew that the next question could be a delicate one. "Miss Bond, as this is a murder enquiry, every avenue has to be explored. So questions of a highly personal nature may be asked."

The eyes went over the glasses. "Fire away, inspector."

"My colleague and I couldn't help noticing before that you were arguing with one of your colleagues. May we ask what that was about?"

She smiled, the wide thin lips somehow becoming wider and thinner. "I assume you're referring to the argument I had with Veronica, Veronica Makepeace. She's my partner."

"I see," said the inspector, with a smile that implied more information was requested.

"This morning, I found her in the office with Rosemary Hepworth, the departmental secretary. They were embracing each other." She held up a hand. "I know now that they had just received news about Delia's murder, and I suppose, on reflection, that I acted and spoke hastily, both then and later. That's all it was about. I believe a student found her."

"Found Dr Bumstead, you mean? Yes, a student called Anne Dickinson. Do you know her?"

The hint of a smile came to her lips. "Oh, her. Oh, yes. I taught her in the first year. A bit of a rough diamond, shall we say. One could never accuse Anne Dickinson of being over-sophisticated."

"Why?"

"Well, the way she speaks."

"You mean she uses inappropriate language?"

"Not in the sense of foul language, no. But there are times when, shall we say, her class background shows itself."

"Oh, I see." *Just as it does in all of us,* he thought. "Anyway, thank you, Miss Bond."

As he and Mark Newport suddenly got up to leave, he thought he saw a tiny flicker of relief on the ice-cool features. He was about to open the door when he suddenly turned around.

"Oh, by the way, Miss Bond, you're a part-time member of staff, aren't you?"

"Yes, that's right."

"Have you ever wanted to become full-time?"

"Well, I did once, but I'm quite happy with the way things are at the moment. Besides, when I saw how nasty Delia was to other colleagues when they wanted to go full-time, I decided it wasn't worth the aggro."

It was somehow amusing to hear the colloquial expression coming from such a cultured voice.

"In what way can you imagine Delia being nasty with you, Miss Bond?"

"Well, she would have made sure that my private life would have been aired to one and all, the students included. I can do without that. Also, Veronica wasn't prepared to stomach it, either." She fixed her eyes on him. "If you're looking for suspects, inspector, you're going to end up with quite a long list, I'm telling you."

Ray Farrar had informed Gillian Taylor and Alan Henry about the heated argument that he and Mark Newport had witnessed between Harriet Bond and Veronica Makepeace. He had also ensured that the two women would be interviewed at the same time, so that one wouldn't be able to forewarn the other about their argument having been overheard. But they were even more interested in what the murdered woman's husband had said about her not having had children, and decided that a pooling of ideas and theories was necessary later in the day.

"Can we start by asking you how you got on with Dr Bumstead, please, Miss Makepeace?" Gillian Taylor smiled as she spoke, in an attempt to put the woman at her ease.

"Well, you see," she said as she suddenly looked over her shoulder furtively and dropped her voice, "I didn't really get on with her." The voice went even lower. "Four walls and all that, of course..."

The police woman knew instinctively that Veronica Makepeace was one of those people who are found in every group – the gossip, the amateur politician. Her very next words gave her away.

"I would never spread anything around, of course..." Another rapid glance over her shoulder followed.

"Of course not, Miss Makepeace. Strictly between ourselves."

"Quite."

"Do go on."

"Well, she used to spread malicious gossip about me – and others. But about me – and Harriet – especially."

"And why did she do that?"

She played with her hands, then swallowed. "Because Harriet and I are partners." A red flush had come to her neck. "But we've always considered that it's our business. We aren't harming anyone."

"Absolutely, Miss Makepeace." Gillian Taylor nodded her head slowly, thinking of one of her colleagues, a decent woman and first-rate officer, whose life was often made a misery for the same reason.

The woman's voice lowered again, her eyes furtively glancing at the door behind her. "Not that Delia was in a position to talk about private morals, of course."

"Why do you say that, Miss Makepeace?"

She played with a large ring on her left hand. "Well, it isn't for me to indulge in gossip, of course…"

"Of course, Miss Makepeace, we understand."

"It would be most unprofessional, anyway…"

"Of course, Miss Makepeace. But, in a situation like this, we want to have as much information as possible, as you can imagine… So, you were saying?"

"Yes, well, Delia didn't have much room to talk where personal morality is concerned…" She tried to keep a mischievous smile under control. "But I once caught her taking a photo of one of the male students as he lay on the grass sunbathing." Her voice by now had become a secretive whisper. "Of course, I don't know why she was taking a photo of him, when there were other male students around…."

"I see. And could you tell me the name of this particular student, Miss Makepeace?"

"Michael Springer."

"The student who was murdered recently?"

She pursed her lips and slowly nodded her head.

"But *two* children, she'd said to Liz Goodwin, Mark. Had she been married before, and her former husband had got custody…"

"Or had she had them when very young, sir?"

"And then got them adopted. Twins, maybe…You're thinking the same as me, Mark… Her extra year at Cumbria University…"

"Yes, that's right, sir. Do you want me to check details of her university career?"

Ray Farrar scratched the back of his neck. "It's a long time ago, now, though, isn't it? Over twenty years..."

"Well, they keep records like that these days, sir – you know, they have departments organising get-togethers for past students."

"Oh, yes, what did my daughter say they're called... Alumni officers, yes, that's it. Alan Henry keeps getting news sheets and journals from where he was a student, doesn't he? Good thinking, Mark. We have her maiden name - Kennedy, her husband said it was. We'll phone Cumbria University after we've seen the next member of staff. Perhaps we could get Gillian or Alan to do it."

It was clear, as they approached Ingrid Kaltz's office, that she was in a rather heated discussion with Jean-Luc Lafarge. Both lecturers had their backs to the policemen.

"Let's edge a little closer, see if there's anything interesting to pick up," murmured Ray Farrar.

"But I have never taught a group at that hour!"

"Jean-Luc, I'm afraid that's tough! You're going to have to do it next year!"

"And why is it *my* hour that has to be changed? Bloody buggery! I bet Terry Trotter's hour isn't changed. Everyone's piss scared of him!"

Ingrid Kaltz raised her voice. "Well *I* am not scared of him, Jean-Luc! I've just been given this job to do as year tutor responsible for the first-year time-table, and as I have never done it before, I'm doing the best I can to fit all the different lectures in without there being any clashes!"

"But if I keep my normal hour, then I can see the same group two hours on the run. I can kill two birds in the one bush!"

"Well, I'm sorry, Jean-Luc, but I've been told that there are to be no double sessions. The hour will have to be changed to Thursday, and starting an hour later!"

"But that would mean me teaching until five o'clock!"

"Well, yes, that's what most staff do, Jean-Luc, people in other jobs work all hours..."

"Well I haven't worked until five o'clock for five or six years! You can't expect me to teach until five o'clock! My nerves won't stand it! When winter comes, it depresses me going home in the dark!"

She stared at him. "What? What world do you live in?"

He stamped his foot. "Ah, yes, here we go! That's the trouble with giving power to a German!"

She exploded, her head jutting forward. "And what does that mean? I'll have you know, my own grandfather died in a German prison camp!"

"How, what happened? Did he fall out of a watchtower?"

As Ingrid stepped towards him, he walked away quickly, then turned and shouted, "They are all the same in this place – they have you by the curly shorts!"

In her annoyance she dropped some papers on the floor, and as she bent down to pick them up, she noticed the two policemen and smiled awkwardly at them. "Hello. I am sorry about that." She opened her office door. "Please come in."

"A trying day for you all, Miss Kaltz," said Ray Farrar, as a conversation opener.

She sighed and put the offending papers into an envelope. "Yes, indeed. Can I get you a coffee, a tea?"

"No, thank you, thanks all the same."

"You see what this place is like? You try and do your job, then you get shouted at, moaned at. That's the trouble with higher education nowadays. You get managers – or so-called managers, an army of them, as Mick says – shouting at you from above, then there are students who know their rights complaining from the other end, and people like Jean-Luc…"

"He does seem to be the nervous type, Miss Kaltz."

She ran her hands through her hair. "Yes, I think *seem* is the operative word, inspector, if you want my opinion."

"What do you mean, exactly, Miss Kaltz?"

"Well, I have been asked to do this new job of being responsible for first-year students and their time-table. So I am busy trying to organise the time-table for next year. It's never the same two years on the run because there are always new options that students can take, or certain options stop running."

"And this new responsibility that you've been given – is it a promotion?"

She threw her fair head back and laughed. "Oh, forgive me, inspector, I do not wish to be rude. No, it is anything but a promotion! I'll get no extra money, only extra hassle! They have allowed me an hour off my teaching, but I know

73

that the extra stress and work involved will take up a lot more than one hour per week."

"I see…"

"They wouldn't ask Jean-Luc to do it, of course. He'd make a mess of it. Anything he's asked to do, he makes a mess of – he *makes sure* he does, so he isn't asked again. You may think it's funny about him not wanting to go home in the dark. But there's something even funnier."

"What's that, Miss Kaltz?"

"He's on the same money as me, as Mick O'Reilly, as Maureen Threlfall."

"I see. Do other staff share your sense of injustice, Miss Kaltz?"

"Oh, yes. There are people here who work like slaves, they deserve double their pay. People like Mick O'Reilly, Maureen Threlfall, Paul Richardson. And Terry Trotter, it has to be said."

"And there are those who don't fall into that category?"

"Oh, yes. And they are always the ones with the most to say. There are people here, like Jean-Luc, who use up more energy in their efforts to avoid work than they'd use up if they did it in the first place! Jean-Luc told me last week that he goes home every night and thinks he's going to die through over-work."

"And you don't share that view?"

"Inspector." Her voice was suddenly much quieter, her whole demeanour much calmer. "From what Jean-Luc's wife once said to me at a party when she'd had a few too many sherries down her, I think Jean-Luc goes home every night and wets himself laughing, knowing that he's fooled everyone for yet another day."

It was clear from the rest of the interview that Ingrid Kaltz had great respect, and even affection, for her head of section, Maureen Threlfall. She also shared Maureen's view of Delia Bumstead, namely that the murdered woman could somehow inspire dislike and pity at the same time.

Ray Farrar had found, as the day wore on, that his interest in the murdered student Michael Springer was slowly becoming an obsession. So he reserved his final question for this.

"Miss Kaltz, how well did you know Michael Springer?"

"Oh, Michael Springer. Not all that well, the poor lad. I only taught him for one year, I think. He spent more time chasing women than studying!"

"I see. That does seem to be his reputation, from all accounts."

The young woman eyed him speculatively. "Do you think that his murder is linked to Delia's, inspector?"

He couldn't help but smile at her directness. "I have no idea, Miss Kaltz. But he was always after the women, you say."

"Oh, yes. One day, I even caught him in the office with his arm around Rosemary's waist. She's the secretary. Almost old enough to be his mother."

"And how did she react?"

She grinned. "She didn't seem to mind, from the smile on her face. And yet it's strange…"

"What is, Miss Kaltz?"

"Well, there was one girl he seemed very keen on, in fact I think they were even living together for a while. Then it all came to nothing, and they ended up not even speaking to each other." She clicked her fingers as it came to her. "Yes, Valerie Salter, that was her name."

Chapter 8

"And she's quite sure that Delia Bumstead was taking a photo of the student called Springer, Gillian?"

"Yes, sir. She seemed absolutely certain that that was what the woman was doing." Gillian Taylor nodded her head vigorously. "It's obvious that the Makepeace woman is a bit of a gossip, but there was no doubt in her mind."

"Well, there's no apparent reason why she should make something like that up, certainly." Ray Farrar crossed one leg over the other. "It gets more interesting by the minute... Anyway, let's discuss Barry Bumstead for a bit, while we wait for Alan. Come on, Gillian, tell us what you think. Is he telling the truth, in that he was totally unaware that his wife had had children? Had she already had children before he knew her, twins perhaps, in the year out that she'd spent while at Cumbria University?" The inspector turned to Mark Newport. "And you've got an interesting theory, too, haven't you, Mark?"

"Well, it could well be that she'd had children when married to Barry Bumstead, but then lost them in infancy – you know, some unusual illness or condition, or whatever..."

"And Barry Bumstead's trying to blank it all out from his mind?" said Gillian Taylor, nodding her head. "Yes, it can happen, I believe. The pain of it all was too much, so it's a form of escapism. Could be."

"Anyway, you've got Susan Barrow next, haven't you? She's Carruthers's colleague in the Geography section, isn't she? I wonder if she's a mad champagne revolutionary as well."

At that very moment, Alan Henry appeared, frowning.

"Sir, we won't be interviewing Susan Barrow, I'm afraid."

"Why's that?"

"The secretary's just told me that she was seeing her doctor this morning, and she's nowhere to be found."

"And no-one's got any idea where she'll be?"

"Apparently she's suffering from depression, and it's not the first time she's done this – the third, in fact. She came in this morning, after she'd seen the doctor, and she was present at the meeting that we called. Then she went missing, it seems. The secretary says that whenever she does this, she drives up to Yorkshire, somewhere up in the Pennines. The secretary says she'll be all right. She'll spend the night in a b-and-b somewhere, then come back tomorrow. That's what she did on the two previous occasions, anyway."

"God, what a bloody place…"

"I've already checked with the surgery, as well, sir. She was there for her appointment, which was at a quarter past eight, but didn't see the doctor until half past because they were running late, and didn't leave the practice until about a quarter to nine. It's also about three miles away from the College."

Ray Farrar nodded. "So that would make it extremely difficult for her to be here when the Bumstead woman was killed."

"Difficult, but not impossible, sir."

"No, you're right." He pulled a face. "OK, we'll interview her when she comes back, first thing tomorrow." He suddenly looked at his watch. "Right, you and Gillian go and interview the secretary, and Mark and I will interview the Head of Department and his side-kick. Then we'll have a long chat afterwards. Dr Bumstead's lost children are interesting me more and more, not to mention the former student called Springer."

Mick O'Reilly had phoned his wife to say that he'd be home a little later than usual because of what had happened at the College. He had said good bye to Paul Richardson, who had asked him if he and his wife Colette fancied coming around for a drink, and was about to get into his car when he noticed that a silver Mercedes was reversing into a parking space.

"You're driving a bit too close to that car, madam," he said to himself. The driver, a woman called Lucy Wendover who was the P.A. of one of the Assistant Directors, manoeuvred the car closer and closer to the back of another car parked in the space directly behind. The owner of the parked car, a pleasant and hardworking third year student called Liz Farne whom Mick expected to do very well in her Finals, watched with horror as the inevitable happened.

"Excuse me," she shouted to the woman in the Mercedes, "you've just bumped my car."

The woman got out and smiled at the girl. "Yes, so what's the problem? I always park like that. Don't you?"

Liz Farne looked at her nonplussed. "Pardon?"

"I always park like that. Everyone does. That's what bumpers are for, aren't they?"

Yes, you bloody arrogant, pompous cow, Mick O'Reilly thought to himself. *You mustn't apologise, must you? Bluster, bluster, bluster, that's the way. Never admit you're in the wrong, never admit you've made a mistake. Is that what they've taught you at the top of the greasy pole? Or perhaps you have to be like that to be interested in going up the greasy pole in the first bloody place...*

By the time he walked across, Liz had finished examining her back bumper.

"Is everything all right, Liz?" he said.

She looked up, obviously flustered. "Oh, hello, Mick. Yes, I think so."

"And what's this got to do with you?" The woman's eyes burned into his.

"I've just witnessed a car hitting another, Mrs Wendover. So it's got quite a bit to do with me. Just as I would be a witness if I saw a car hit yours."

"Don't you know the word sorry?" Liz asked the woman, a little more confident now that Mick was on the scene.

"There's no damage done, so there's no need to say sorry."

"Well, Mrs Wendover, surely the principle is that you should say sorry whether there's damage done or not." He returned her icy glare with an artificial smile. "Well, of course, that's what I was always taught." He looked her up and down before adding, with the same fixed smile, "But, then again, I suppose we are all the product of how our parents brought us up, aren't we?"

The woman, her face now crimson, moved her mouth as though about to say something, then got into her car and drove away, the tyres screeching as she turned a corner near some terrified students.

"What a horrible, rude woman! Anyway, thank you, Mick. I'm grateful for your support."

"That's all right, Liz, no problem. It was her attitude, more than anything, which got me."

"Yes, that's right. Why couldn't she say sorry?"

"Presumably because she isn't big enough, Liz."

The girl smiled as she got into her Ford Fiesta, waving to him as she drove off. He then got into his car and sat at the wheel for a few seconds, watching the rain patter against the windscreen and thinking about the woman's rudeness. But he was also intrigued as to why she had a letter that had been posted to the house of Eric Fisher, the Assistant Head of Department, lying on the passenger seat.

"Are you any further with your investigation yet, inspector?"

Ray Farrar scrutinised the Head of Department before speaking. "Well, progress is slow, Dr Cassidy, but we're confident of getting there. We were wondering if you or Dr Fisher could give us any details, any details at all, on Dr Bumstead and her relations with the staff."

Eric Fisher signalled to the Head of Department to begin the proceedings. Harold Cassidy duly cleared his throat. "Well, far be it from me to cast aspersions, as it were, but, all things considered, and this is a view which I am sure will be shared by many, when all is said and done...."

Ray Farrar's mind went back to his schooldays, where he had a Chemistry teacher who was so boring, so lacking in any basic sparkle, that he would sit in class and watch the man's mouth move without taking in anything of what he was saying. Sitting in the Head of Department's spacious office, he knew he was in danger of having the same experience. He felt that in the middle of all this, Harold Cassidy could well have said something like "East Fife 2, Queen of the South 2" without anyone really noticing. The inspector had to change position frequently to keep focused on what the man was saying. He would come to what Ray Farrar expected to be the end of a sentence, only to suddenly add on two or three clauses or phrases. *If this is how you teach, your students must be asleep after five or ten minutes,* he thought. A glance at Mark Newport's glazed eyes told him that the man was having the same soporific effect on him.

From Harold Cassidy's labyrinthine amble through the English language, they were able to deduce that his feelings for Dr Delia Bumstead coincided with those of everyone else with the exception of Liz Goodwin. As one particularly rambling sentence petered out, Ray Farrar cut in.

"How did Dr Bumstead get on with her students, Dr Cassidy?"

79

The man looked at him blankly for a few seconds. "Students? Oh, them. Oh, all right, from what I could see. We always keep our fingers on the pulse, don't we, Eric?"

Eric Fisher nodded earnestly, then began to speak. It suddenly became clear to both police officers that they were in the presence of a master of oratory, a man in whose hands words were the subtlest of tools. Listening to him speak was what it must have been like watching Michelangelo paint, both men agreed afterwards. The rise and fall of the voice, the occasional hand movements, the breadth of vocabulary and conciseness of expression – all were evidence of a person who was supremely intelligent. *And supremely clever when it suits,* thought Ray Farrar as he viewed the practised smiles of empty charm.

After ten minutes or so, the inspector brought up the topic of Michael Springer's murder. It was Harold Cassidy who spoke first.

"A terrible shock to all the staff, inspector. Personal rivalries and dislikes were temporarily forgotten."

"Personal rivalries, you say. Are there many personal rivalries in the department, Dr Cassidy?"

"Oh good heavens, no. This is a very happy ship. People get on with each other famously."

"It must have been an awful shock especially to those who had taught him," said Eric Fisher. "It is to be hoped that the person or persons responsible are caught. I believe enquiries are still ongoing."

"I take it from what you've said that you didn't teach him, Dr Fisher?"

"No, this is my first year here. Michael Springer left two years ago, I believe. Even if I had been here then, the chances of my having taught him would be slim, as I only teach four hours a week, because of my many onerous administrative and managerial responsibilities. I only wish I could teach a lot more hours, but such is life." He held out his hands and gave a world-weary smile.

"Did you teach him, Dr Cassidy?"

"I'm not sure, actually…"

"I see. We believe he had a reputation for the ladies, to put not too fine a point on it. Can you tell us if there was any student in particular that he formed a relationship with?"

"Er, well, from what I can remember, he seemed very taken with a student called Valerie someone. Nurse Richmond in the Student Health Centre used to always mention it."

"I see."

"From what I've heard about the poor lad since the report of his death, he was very taken with many female students, Harold." Eric Fisher smiled at his colleague and then at the policemen. He suddenly shook his head. "A terrible business, though. You just don't imagine that someone so young can meet such an untimely end. It must have been dreadful for his family."

"There is one member of staff we have been unable to interview, Dr Cassidy, Dr Fisher, and that's someone called Susan Barrow." Mark Newport then sat back in his chair and raised an eyebrow at each of them in turn, as a silent request for comment.

"Yes, poor Susan has her problems, hasn't she, Eric?"

The man sighed. "Oh yes, one can only concur with that sad assessment, unfortunately. Depression, you know." He turned to his colleague. "This isn't the first time, either, I believe, Harold?"

"Oh, no, that's very true. She had it before you came, Eric." He shook his head sadly. "She lets things get to her, you see. I mean, I know we all feel that everything is pressing down on us at times, but poor Susan does tend to take things to heart. I suppose it's in her nature."

"Yes, she's extremely conscientious," said Eric Fisher. He removed his glasses and polished them, shaking his head sadly as he did so. "Between us and the four walls, gentlemen, there are some staff here who could take a few lessons from Susan, some staff who just aren't conscientious enough, sadly."

"I see," said the inspector. "Could you give us a few examples of the sort of things that she lets get at her?"

"Well, it does have to be said that Dr Bumstead has, er, has had a hand in it, shall we say, a few times."

Ray Farrar changed his sitting position. "Such as, Dr Fisher?"

"Well, one doesn't wish to spread gossip, of course... But the most recent occasion, and it's probably the thing which has sparked off Susan's recent crisis, was when Susan was approached a few months ago by the University of the Pennines, who asked her if she would like to be their external examiner in

Geography for four years. That's the usual period."

"And what happened?"

"Well, Susan suddenly received a letter from the University of the Pennines informing her that they were withdrawing their invitation, on the grounds that her teaching experience wasn't considered adequate enough."

"So what has that got to do with Dr Bumstead?"

"Susan was distraught. So she phoned the university, and discovered that Dr Bumstead had contacted one of the staff there and told them she didn't think Susan had the right experience."

"But Geography wasn't Dr Bumstead's speciality." Ray Farrar looked at the two men in turn.

"True, inspector," said Eric Fisher with a knowing smile, "but Delia always poked her nose into every subject, every section. Presumably she'd heard about the invitation to Susan from some source or other… and decided to act, shall we say. I sometimes thought that Delia worked for MI5 on the quiet, such was her ability to sniff out anything about people."

And did she pay for it by being murdered? Ray Farrar asked himself as he sat in thought for a few seconds. He also refrained from asking the Head of Department as to why she had been allowed to do such things without being disciplined, but limited himself to asking a final question.

"And when did Susan Barrow receive the letter from the university, informing her of the change of mind?"

"Last Friday, inspector," said Eric Fisher.

"So presumably she would have found out about Dr Bumstead's intervention on the same day?"

"I suppose so, yes."

Rosemary Hepworth tugged nervously at the thin bracelet on her right hand, her eyes staring and fearful.

"Mrs Hepworth, we realise all this must be an awful shock to you, but we'd be really grateful for any piece of information about Dr Bumstead that you can give us, no matter how small it may seem to be."

"Fine." Another tug at the bracelet.

Gillian Taylor tried to smile reassuringly at the secretary. "First of all, can you tell me how you got on with her?"

"Well, all right, I suppose." She swallowed and gave the bracelet another tug. "I tried to avoid her, to be honest, because I knew how difficult she could be."

"Difficult in what way, Mrs Hepworth?"

"Well, you know, fussy, always wanting her typing to be done before anyone else's. I never had words with her, but I could see why others often did."

"I'm sorry to have to ask this, and I don't want you to feel that you're telling tales, Mrs Hepworth, but are there any staff who seemed to get on especially badly with Dr Bumstead?"

"Well..." She bit her lip and looked down at her bracelet.

"All this will be in the strictest confidence, Mrs Hepworth, we do assure you," said Alan Henry.

"Well, she always had arguments with Terry Trotter, you know, real ding-dongers, out in the open. It even happened once or twice here in the office. It was awful, really embarrassing."

"I see. Anyone else?"

"Well, yes... With Lucinda Hobbs-Smithers and Dominic Carruthers. She had arguments with everyone, really."

"How did she get on with Susan Barrow?"

"Badly. She used to make nasty comments about Susan being off work with her nerves and about her drinking a lot."

"I see," said Gillian Taylor, momentarily embarrassed as she thought of her hangover. "Was there anyone on the staff that she did get on with?"

"Liz Goodwin. They seemed to get on quite well. Delia always seemed that bit more relaxed whenever she spoke to her. They sometimes went for a coffee together, that sort of thing."

"How did Dr Bumstead get on with the Head and Assistant Head of Department, Mrs Hepworth?"

"Well, at meetings she used to complain that the department lacked direction, that things were being left that should have been seen to. She used to make things quite difficult for Dr Cassidy."

"In what way?"

"Well, if ever she stirred things up between staff, they'd come to him and start complaining. And she would often go to some of the Assistant Directors and tell them that things were not being done properly in the department. That made things really difficult for Dr Cassidy."

"I see. And how did she get on with Dr Fisher?"

She sat and thought for a few seconds. She seemed so deep in thought that her body visibly relaxed. "Well, it isn't for me to say, but she never seemed to speak to him. Not that he's been here all that long."

"You mean, here, in the office, they wouldn't exchange a word?"

"Well, they'd say hello or good morning, and that was it, as far as I can remember. I think he tried to avoid her as much as possible."

"Was this because of a previous row that they'd had?" asked Alan Henry.

"Probably. Well, I suppose I shouldn't say that, because I don't really know. I know she was often scathing about him."

"In what way?"

"Well, I heard Delia complain about him once or twice, saying that he never seemed to be around when he was needed, that sort of thing. But Delia was like that, really. She always found someone to get at. Mick O'Reilly always said that she could start an argument in an empty house."

"Mrs Hepworth," said Gillian Taylor, "how did Dr Bumstead get on with the students?"

"Not bad, from what I could make out, though once or twice you could hear them moaning about how strictly she marked their work."

"From what we can deduce, it would seem that Dr Bumstead had enemies, for want of a better word, among the staff. Are there any students that you know of who disliked her intensely?"

"Not really, no. Not enough to…" She shook her head and bit her lip.

"How did she get on with Michael Springer?"

Another tug at the bracelet. "Oh, poor Michael. I think she got on with him the same as with all the others, I suppose… She always said that if he'd been as interested in his work as he was in girls, he'd have done extremely well."

"Oh, yes," said Gillian Taylor. "He was a young man for the girls, so we're led to believe. Did he have any girlfriend in particular… you know, anyone that seemed to stand out among the rest?"

"Well, there was one… a girl called Valerie Salter. He seemed to be with her a lot. That's all I know, really."

But it isn't all you know, there's something you're not telling us, thought Gillian as she moved to get out of her chair to signal the end of the interview.

Chapter 9

"So we're all agreed that the only person in the place *not* to have had a good reason for killing her seems to be Liz Goodwin, then?"

Ray Farrar's three colleagues, their elbows resting on a round table, nodded sombrely.

"There are some staff who seem to stand out more than others, though, sir," said Gillian Taylor. "What I mean is, there are some who seem to have a bigger motive than others."

"Yes, perhaps," said her boss, "though from what we know of her, she seems to have had an endless list of enemies." The inspector started counting on his fingers. "We know from the guy called Bent that she went to the high-ups telling tales about the people she worked with. That's enough to give us a long list of people who'd want to do her in, for a start. And she was responsible for Susan Barrow not being appointed as an external examiner at the University of the Pennines. And there's probably loads of other mischief that she got up to that we don't know about." He examined the fax in front of him that had been sent from the University of Cumbria. "There's nothing on this to suggest anything, no other name in the student year group that rings any bells with names here. Not that I was optimistic about it being as easy as that in the first place. And her year out says just that – a year out."

"The business about the student called Springer fascinates me, sir," said Gillian Taylor. "There's something that the secretary wasn't telling Alan and me – we could both sense it. Didn't Ingrid Kaltz say that she caught Springer with his arm around Rosemary Hepworth in the office one day, and she didn't seem to be protesting?"

"OK, so maybe Mrs Hepworth has a jealous husband who hears of it? Is it enough for him to go to Manchester and kill him – especially what must be a couple of years after the event?"

Gillian Taylor immediately nodded her head in agreement with Mark Newport's rejection of her line of thought. "No, you're right, Mark. From the sound of him, the Springer lad must have annoyed quite a few males in his time. We've got to be careful to distinguish information from gossip. But what I am saying is that she was very nervous, she was keeping something from us."

"OK, Gillian, we'll work on her again tomorrow. But are we right to be thinking that it was because of jealousy that the lad was killed?" said Ray Farrar, partly to himself.

"You mean that his murder has something to do with the fact that he was a student here, sir, rather than his attempted sexual conquests?"

"Exactly, Mark. The more I think about it, the more convinced I am that Dr Bumstead's murder and Michael Springer's murder are linked in some way."

"With both murders done by the same person, sir?"

"Possibly, Alan. If that is the case, then it might make our job that bit easier. But what if it's more complex than that?" He yawned and rubbed his eyes. "Come on, we'll call it a day. If any of you come up with anything, or a sudden idea comes to you, let me know. As long as it's during half time – there's a good match on the telly tonight. And I've got my son's under-15s match on Sunday to arrange. That and a couple of beers after a day here will do me fine, I think…"

Anne Dickinson was tired, very tired. It was a tiredness that had suddenly come upon her, delayed shock after what she had been through, was Geraldine Murphy's opinion when Anne had a spare minute to ring her on her mobile between serving customers and clearing tables. She looked at her watch. Half past seven. Not too long to go, she thought, then I'll be back at the flat. She was about to carry some dirty mugs into the washing area when she noticed that the young woman had returned, the one that nurse Richmond had recognised when she had been in the cafe earlier. What was her name, nurse Richmond said? Valerie something – Valerie Salter, that was it. What was strange was that nurse Richmond had suddenly become preoccupied, miles away, when she had realized who the young woman was, which was most unlike her.

There was something certainly strange about the young woman, the look in her eyes, especially. They were intense, searching. They were eyes that seemed to stare through things and not just look at them.

Her eyes devoured the menu, which she then tossed to one side on the table before turning her attention to the rain that had just started to hammer against the window. All her movements seemed jerky, tense, exaggerated. When the rain subsided into a monotonous drizzle after a minute or so, she noticed a newspaper on the next table that a previous customer had left. It was the local evening newspaper, which Anne had already glanced at, though she had only had time to see the pictures and headlines.

The whole of the front page was given over to the murder. The headline *Parkdale College Murder* took up almost half the page space, photographs of the College and the victim taking up the rest. Readers were invited to read the full in-depth exclusive on pages two and three.

The girl reached across to pick up the newspaper and looked at the front page. Her eyes opened wide, and she put a hand to her mouth to stifle a scream. Her body became rigid and the colour drained from her face. Then she scraped back her chair and raced out of the restaurant, knocking over another chair in the process. She ran straight across the road without looking at the traffic, a car having to screech to a halt to avoid hitting her, its angry horn loud and long.

Anne watched her disappear up a nearby side street, shaking her head in disbelief, then walked across to the table where the newspaper had been left, and picked it up. She went to page two to read the report.

The unthinkable happened at Parkdale College today when the bloodstained body of Dr Delia Bumstead, lecturer in English, was found slumped across her desk in her study. The gruesome discovery was made by a student called Angela Dickinson...

"Grief, can't they even get my name right...?"

Colleagues expressed their shock and horror at this callous murder of a very popular member of staff. Dr Harold Cassidy, Head of the Department of Social and Language Studies, said that she was a shining example of all that a friend and colleague should be. "She was always co-operative, always selfless and ready to help others. It is a privilege to have worked with her," he said, obviously moved. Dr Eric Fisher, Assistant Head of Department, echoed these sentiments, saying, "I will never forget the depth of her kindness and the warmth of her friendship." Mr Cuthbert Bent, Assistant Director (Personnel), said that Dr Bumstead's input will be sadly missed. "She is totally and utterly irreplaceable," he said, and added, "We hope to appoint her successor in a week or two's time."...Police have been combing the campus for clues and interviewing members of staff...Nigel Jevons, widely touted as the next President of the Student Union, spoke of his sheer disbelief at this outrage, while also expressing the hope that for the good of the students the College would replace Dr Bumstead with someone matching her academic quality ...

"Two quiche and chips, please..."

Anne let the newspaper fall onto the table and looked around. "Oh, I'm sorry..."

An elderly lady smiled at her. "Don't worry, love. Two quiche and chips, please, and two coffees. Both with milk, one with two sugars, one without." She pointed to the headline in the newspaper. "Terrible, isn't it? I don't know what things are coming to."

An elderly man with thick glasses at a nearby table agreed, wiping tomato ketchup from most of his mouth. "The times we're living in, eh, love? Mind you, I've always said they should bring back national service."

"Aye, you're dead right there. A couple of years in the army would soon sort them out."

"And all this European business is to blame, as well, if you ask me," said her companion, taking a soaking plastic cover off her head. "Euro this, Euro that – it's ridiculous. I mean, it's disgusting the way all foreigners are out of step with the British – they all drive on the wrong side of the road, they aren't C of E, they don't eat meat with two veg. The weather's never been the same since we joined this European thing, either."

"Well, I blame the teachers, like, myself personally," said a woman who was paying her bill. "Six weeks holiday a year, they're finished by about half three in the afternoon. Or they go on study trips with the kids. That must be a relaxing day out for them. Cushy, or what, eh? And all they do is moan."

"Women being educated. That's the reason for all our problems, if you ask me," said a military looking man with a thin black moustache. "In the old days, women knew their place. Not now. All this equality rubbish – it turns people's minds. It said so in the paper, so it must be right."

"Yes, you're dead right there, love..."

Ray Farrar was standing by the car, waiting for Mark Newport, who had gone to the toilet. The rain had stopped and the sun had reappeared, though the lawns and trees were soaking, and a mass of cloud behind the hills hinted at more rain to come. There was a faint smell of food from the refectory in the student union, a smell that became stronger as the inspector walked towards the side of the building, where a notice about his younger daughter's favourite local band had caught his attention. The notice said that the band was going to perform at some venue in the town later that month. He made a mental note of it as he turned back towards the car, idly wondering if his daughter knew about the concert.

At that very moment, Rosemary Hepworth came out of a door at the side of the main building. He hadn't noticed the door before, thinking that the only doors to the building were at the front and back. Then he realised that the location of the door meant that it was virtually next to the secretary's office, and was presumably one she normally used. As she came out, she half turned and said something to someone who was coming out of the building behind her. It was nurse Richmond.

What immediately caught his interest was that the nurse was obviously distressed. The two women hadn't noticed him, and were walking away from him. The secretary put her arm around the nurse's shoulder as they turned a corner towards a car park reserved for staff, and when the two women were out of sight he walked briskly towards the corner of the building to get nearer to them. Their voices, while low, were quite audible.

"Amy, now stop upsetting yourself, you'll only make yourself ill. There's nothing you can do about it."

"But I'll always feel I didn't do enough to help her, Rosemary... And then look at what she ended up doing... I tried to advise her ..."

"Exactly, Amy. You tried to advise her, and she took no notice of you. Because she was being pressurised by him. But that isn't your fault. You've got to stop blaming yourself."

The two women started walking again, and the inspector was wondering whether he should follow them or not, when a loud voice behind him not only made him turn around but also alerted the secretary and the nurse to the fact that he was behind them.

"Hello, inspector. Must be very interesting work, snooping around, listening to other people's conversations. I suppose we'll be seeing you and your colleagues here again tomorrow, no doubt."

Lucinda Hobbs-Smithers gave a malicious and knowing grin as she pointed her car keys towards a silver BMW bearing a private number plate and a sticker in the back window encouraging people to join the Socialist Workers Party.

"Mick said could he and Colette come around tonight, or we could go there if we can get a baby-sitter."

Helen Richardson pulled a face as she checked a boiling pan. "Well, I doubt if I'll get someone at this short notice. I can try, though."

Paul waved a hand. "No, let's have them around here, it'll be easier all round. We haven't had them here for about a month, anyway. We'll try and get the kids to bed by seven."

After phoning Mick, Paul set the table. Talk throughout the evening meal was devoted entirely to Delia Bumstead's murder. Paul tried to remember as much detail as possible, although his account was bitty, jumbled, as his mind jumped from one thing to another.

"Oh, I'm not making sense," he said, staring at the potato on his fork, as he contradicted himself on something he had said previously.

"Nothing to do with that place makes any sense," said Helen. "I've never known such a group of peculiar people in one place. It's as if fate, or whatever, has put together the strangest people imaginable just to see what they all come up with. How people like you, Mick and Maureen keep your sanity there, I don't know. I sometimes wish you'd stayed at the high school."

"Well, the students are normal – well, most of them are. There's that to be thankful for. I love the teaching bit."

She put down her knife and fork onto her empty plate. "Yes, but you're not even left in peace to do that, are you? Look at the amount of paperwork that keeps getting passed on to you. And what for? To justify the existence of the so-called managers who in turn want to justify their ridiculous salaries. You can't do your preparation and marking properly because some genius will have invented some meeting or other, where people can get hot under the collar and fling insults at each other, criticising each other. I think some of them actually enjoy it!"

"Oh, I'm sure you're right. Eric Fisher was late for the meeting that the police called this morning, as well. He sauntered in after it had started, large as life."

She snorted and shook her head. "Surprise, surprise! You know why he was late? Because he was in the betting-shop in town! Even Thomas noticed him going in! It's unbelievable what that man gets away with. And what gets me is, he seems to do it openly, blatantly. Hasn't anyone ever tackled him about it?"

"Not tackled him about it as such, no, but Terry Trotter once bumped into him, literally, as he was coming out of the betting shop one day. Terry asked him what he'd been doing in there."

"And what did he say?"

"He said he was doing research into people's behaviour when they put a bet on and listen to the commentary. A psychological study of impulse and expectation, I think his words were."

"Good grief. And I bet he said it without batting an eyelid."

"Oh, yes, he will have, knowing Fisher."

"That's the trouble with these people, I think they tell lies to themselves as much as they tell lies to others." She took the cloth off the table and folded it in half. "They are a funny lot, though, aren't they? I mean, with the exception of Mick and Maureen, how many people in that place would you keep in touch with if you were to leave tomorrow?"

"I know what you mean... By the way, Frances McAteer's pregnant."

Her eyes lit up. "Oh, that's fantastic news! Marvellous! Now she's nice, really nice, but you tend to forget about her." She nodded her head. "Yes, it's only the nutcases in that place that you tend to remember, not the ordinary sane people." She threw a paper serviette into a bin under the sink. "You know what I mean, though. I can never see many of them ever relax, ever be themselves. Look at that Hobbs-Smithers one, who goes on about the class system. What in God's name does she know about the working classes? And there's Rosemary Hepworth – she's nice enough, she's never done me any harm, but she's one of those people who were thirty-five when they were born."

The dish-washer had just been stacked and the first moves made for getting the children to bed, when the phone rang. Helen gave a wry smile as she spoke into the mouthpiece. "Well, if you've managed to get a baby-sitter, Julie, come around! The more the merrier, as they say!"

"What's that?" he said as she replaced the receiver.

"That was Julie," she said with a grin. "She and Mark are coming around for a drink, as well."

Paul laughed. "I wonder what we'll spend the evening talking about?"

"So Paul wasn't embarrassed by you being there today, then?"

Mark Newport gently removed his daughter's filthy bib. "Ray Farrar had asked me the same thing. No, you know what Paul's like. He knows there's a job to be done. If anything, I was the one who felt a bit uncomfortable, you know, asking Paul and his colleague questions. But Paul was good about it."

"What's Paul's boss like? Helen always says he's very nice."

"Yes, I like him. I took to him right away - a scouser called O'Reilly. He seems to have his head screwed on and to live in the real world."

"Helen always says there are some nutters there, though."

"Oh, there are. I can see now what Paul means whenever he goes on about the place. One idiot was spouting about when the revolution comes, then some pushy bitch was mouthing off to Gillian about how she knew her rights, there's some Belgian bloke who seems a bag of nerves and gets his English all mixed up, one of the women who teaches Geography has flipped and gone missing for the second or third time, the Head of Department doesn't seem to have a clue, the Assistant Head is a sciver but plausible with it. Oh, and we came across one of the high ups who appeared to be a first class pillock with distinction."

"Which is presumably why he's one of the high ups. How does Paul deal with all that?"

"Well, there are some normal people there – the bloke called O'Reilly, two women called Maureen Threlfall and Frances McAteer. Oh, and there's a German woman called Ingrid something who seems quite sensible. She was having an argument with the Belgian bloke who was upset because she'd put him down to teach until five o'clock."

His wife's eyes narrowed. "Well why couldn't he teach until five o'clock?"

"Wait for it." He grinned. "Because it depresses him in winter going home in the dark."

She folded her arms and looked out at the garden, slowly shaking her head. "How in God's name would he get on teaching twenty-seven or twenty-eight five year olds? How would he cope with a sobbing five year old whose grandparent had been buried the day before?"

The phone rang. Julie picked it up. "Oh, hello, Mr Farrar. No, it's OK, we've finished eating. He's here now."

"Hello, sir." Julie went on looking out at the rain gently soaking the garden, then turned sharply at her husband's sudden intake of breath. "What? Now that could be really interesting. I wonder why she wrote to her?... Yes, absolutely... OK, sir, I'll pick you up tomorrow at eight thirty."

"What was that about?"

"Well, you know the bloke I mentioned who was preaching revolution and so on? He said that a girl who used to be a student at the College had phoned him to see if she could speak to him this morning, but hadn't said what it was about. He'd arranged to meet her in a coffee bar in town, but she didn't turn up. Well, they've been going through the murdered woman's office, and they've found a letter written by the same girl to the murdered woman, asking her if she could see her."

"So there could be some link somewhere..."

"Yes, but the other thing is, this girl used to go out with a lad who was a student there who was found murdered in Manchester recently..."

"So the two murders are linked?"

"We don't know. We're not sure as yet. I can tell that Ray Farrar thinks they are in some way."

"Or the girl who used to be a student there is some way linked to the two murders as well?"

"We don't know that, either."

She laughed and kissed him on the cheek. "You can't fool me, I know you too well! You think there's a link between the two murders *and* the girl."

Chapter 10

She sat at the bar and swished the red wine around, noting how it made patterns on the inside of the glass. The Pennine wind suddenly hurled rain against the window to her right, and a young man who came into the bar was soaked, his dark hair matted to his head.

"And this is supposed to be nearly summer, eh," he said to her as he took his raincoat off and put it on a hook attached to the wall.

She smiled and nodded but said nothing, her eyes returning to her almost empty wineglass. She drained the glass and held it up to the barman in a silent request for a refill. She'd had two glasses already. *You need to be careful,* she told herself as she watched the poured wine slowly caress the side of the glass. *You don't want to go down that road again...Just because you feel depressed...*

She went to take a sip of the replenished glass, but instead took out her mobile phone and looked at it intently for a few moments before dialling a number.

"Hi, Rosemary, it's me... I hope you don't mind me calling you at home... Yes, I'm OK, thanks, honestly... Well, things just got on top of me yet again.... I know, I couldn't believe it when I heard about it... Well, it could be anyone, couldn't it?... Well, we all know what sort of a person she was, but it's still an awful thing to happen... I suppose the police will think that I've got something to do with it because I've gone missing... What did you say to them when you realised I wasn't there?... Oh, OK, fine. Thanks, Rosemary... Well, Delia's the reason I have gone missing, really.... Well, it's about my appointment as External at The Pennines University. I'll tell you about it when I get back... Yes, I'll be back tomorrow. I'm staying the night in Yorkshire, at a pub just outside Skipton... Yes, I'll leave here early, then I should be in the College by about half nine or ten... Bobby? Oh, he's fine, he's with my neighbour. She loves looking after him and taking him for walks... OK, Rosemary, see you tomorrow, and thanks for listening. Bye."

She put the mobile into her handbag and gulped down a good portion of the wine that had been placed in front of her. *What a way to celebrate your birthday,* she thought as she repositioned herself on the bar stool.

"Your meal's ready, Miss Barrow."

She drained her glass, then turned to the landlord's daughter and smiled. "Thank you. Could I please have a half bottle of the house red to go with it?"

Frances McAteer and her husband Gerry had left the house to go to work before the post arrived that morning. During the afternoon, Frances had telephoned her husband to tell him about the murder at the College and to say that she might be home later than usual because of all the inquiries the police would have to make. So she promised to let him know when he could come and pick her up at the College, which turned out to be about half an hour later than normal.

When they arrived home, she sifted through the mail that had been waiting on the doormat, then checked to see if any e-mails had come. There was only one, from a former student at the college, Kevin Lomax, whom she remembered as a very thoughtful and serious-minded young man. A little too serious at times, she had always thought, someone who should unwind a bit.

She read the message quickly. It was a request for a reference. Kevin had also sent as an attachment details of the job he was applying for, presumably so that Frances would shape her letter of recommendation to suit the requirements of the post. However, as some of the details seemed a little vague, and as she wanted to help him as much as possible, she thought it would be better to phone him later in the evening, after eating.

The other interesting thing about Kevin Lomax, apart from him being a very pleasant and considerate person, she thought an hour or so later as she put a forkful of plaice to her lips, was that he used to be the best friend of Michael Springer before they had a major fall-out. So as not to miss Coronation Street, she decided to phone Kevin immediately after the meal.

"Hello, Kevin Lomax."

She smiled into the mouthpiece. "Hello, Kevin, it's Frances McAteer here. It was good to hear from you... Of course I don't mind!... I know, I can't believe it, it's dreadful. It's all over the local paper. I suppose it'll be in all the papers tomorrow. Oh yes, the police have been at the College all day... I bet it's been an awful shock for you, too... Well, let's hope so... Anyway, tell me all your news, and what this job's all about..."

She jotted down various details, and smiled up at her husband as he put a coffee on a small table next to her.

"Any news this end? Yes, Kevin, there is. Apart from the awful news about Delia, I've got some news of my own. I'm expecting a baby."

Her husband saw her eyes fill up as Kevin spoke from the other end. "Oh, that's lovely of you, Kevin... Ooh, do tell her, yes. Do you often see her, then?...Really! Good for you! She's a lovely girl! Let's hope things develop, as they say!... Well, I know Michael's death must have been a dreadful shock to you... You and he were very close friends, weren't you, at one stage... Well, I knew you and he had a big fall-out... Oh, over Valerie, oh, I see. That's a coincidence, she was seen at the College and in town today... Well, I know she and Michael had been an item, to use the phrase... What?... Oh my God, Kevin, never... Oh, that's awful. So that was why you fell out?... Well, yes, I can see why...Oh, dear..."

Her husband looked on concerned as her voice became a little shaky. Within a few seconds, a tear was running down her cheek.

"Well, yes, perhaps you're right, Kevin. Perhaps you should tell the police, given the circumstances. They're very discreet when they have to be, I'm sure..."

A few minutes later, her husband's arm around her shoulder, she was on the phone to Maureen Threlfall, her closest friend on the staff. She animatedly recounted her phone conversation with Kevin Lomax, and Maureen agreed with her that in the circumstances it would be advisable to speak with Inspector Farrar first thing the following morning.

No sooner had Mark and Julie Newport sat down when there was another knock on the door. Paul opened it to find Mick and Colette O'Reilly on the doorstep, collars turned up against the rain. Mick held a bottle of wine in one hand and a four-pack in the other.

Introductions were made, and before any embarrassed silence could descend, Mick O'Reilly said what was in everybody's mind as Paul passed him a beer glass.

"Well, what a day, eh? I still can't believe what's happened."

"I'm sure nobody can, Mick," said Helen Richardson.

"In one horrible way, though," said Colette O'Reilly, "that place is so crazy that it isn't really all that surprising." She held up a hand. "Don't get me wrong. I'm not being callous. What's happened is absolutely dreadful, we all know that. But if there was a College in the country where such a thing could have happened, it could only be Parkdale College."

"I know what you mean, Colette." Paul Richardson passed a plate of crisps over to his wife and Julie Newport, who were sharing the settee. "I've been there now almost a year, but I still come home feeling shell-shocked at times."

"It makes you wonder if there are other places which are the same, though, doesn't it?" Mick O'Reilly wiped a thin line of froth from his upper lip as he put down his beer. "I was external examiner at St Barnabas's University College, and there was a gang of nutters there."

"In what way?" asked Mark Newport, grinning.

"Well, I used to look at the students' exam scripts, to see how the marking had been done, that sort of thing. And one year there had been an almighty row between two members of staff because one of them said that some student should be given fifty-one per cent, and the other said fifty-two." He held out his hands. "What the hell does it matter, when the student's passed, and the marks are in the same classification? Apparently, the two people concerned have never spoken to each other since. Whenever they have to contact each other, they do it by written notes or e-mails. And they share the same office. Absolutely bloody stupid."

"There just isn't time for that sort of nonsense in school teaching," said Julie Newport, to nods of agreement from the other women. "You're too busy chasing your own tail all day long. If you teach in a poor area, you're doing social work rather than teaching half of the time, trying to teach kids from horrendous backgrounds, from homes where people couldn't care about how they do at school."

"And if you teach in a well-to-do area, then you sometimes have the other extreme where parents are concerned," said Helen Richardson, "the pushy articulate parents who know their rights and complain about the slightest thing. Their little darlings are angels and geniuses who can do no wrong. And if they don't get to Oxford to do Nuclear Physics or whatever, then it's your fault for not having taught them properly when they were little. Not everyone's like that, of course. But the few who are like that are a real pain."

"Why are we working in education, eh?" said Mick O'Reilly, reaching across to his pint.

"Well, I suppose people join it for the best of motives," said his wife. "But there are times when you question your own sanity for having devoted your professional life to it. I suppose the good people you meet in it make it all worthwhile."

"That reminds me," said Helen. "I met Jim Gregory in town this morning. He's a lovely bloke, isn't he? I was doing all I could not to cry when he was talking about Edith."

"Yes," said Mick. "It doesn't look too good."

"Jim was talking about how he used to worry himself almost sick about things when he worked at the College, having sleepless nights, dreading certain meetings, that sort of thing. He said that it's only now that he sees how silly it all was and how stupid he was for getting wrapped up in it."

Mick O'Reilly nodded. "You can't help it though, can you? You know things are wrong, you know certain people are a pain in the backside, but you don't say anything to avoid aggro."

"It's only when you get older, maybe, that you can step back and relax a bit more," said his wife.

"That's right," said Mick. "Speaking of Jim Gregory, I always remember what Jean-Luc once said to him when Jim was worried about something. In his inimitable style, and probably getting a couple of phrases wrong, he said, 'Jim, when we both leave here, I will be remembered for a week, and you for a fortnight'."

"Jean-Luc summed it all up perfectly there," said Helen, laughing. "No matter how conscientious you are, or how much of a sciver you are, you're soon forgotten about. Those at the top are only out for their own ends."

"I'll always remember Tina Higgins," said Mick. "Way before your time, Paul. She was secretary to one of the Assistant Directors. She used to come in on a Saturday or Sunday, believe it or not, with a special key, to do some work."

"Why did she do that?"

"Because she lived, ate, drank and breathed the damn place, Helen. Everything seemed to go through her. Then one morning, just like today, Rosemary came up to me and said, 'Mick, I've got some awful news. Tina Higgins is dead'. And do you know what? I had the most ridiculous thought. I thought Tina Higgins *can't* be dead, otherwise Parkdale College wouldn't be functioning. But she *was* dead – she'd died suddenly over the weekend - and Parkdale College went on functioning, and the advert for her job was in the paper the day before her funeral. Nobody is indispensable."

"And who gives Tina Higgins the slightest thought now?"

"Nobody, Helen."

Colette turned to her husband. "And having the likes of Delia in the English section didn't exactly make the job stress-free, did it?"

"It certainly didn't. She *would* have to be in the English section, wouldn't she? Just my bloody luck." He raised a forefinger as a sign of thanks as Paul placed another can by his empty glass. "When I look back now at how I used to worry and let myself get stressed, I feel awful about it. The kids must have seen me as a worrier, as someone permanently uptight. It can spoil your home life if you let it. It's awful, really." He looked across at Mark Newport. "But I suppose any job can be like that, yours as well."

The policeman smiled and, nodding his head in the direction of his wife, said, "Well, I am told off for bringing the job home with me at times, I must admit."

"And do you get any thanks for it? Are you appreciated more for it?" said Julie Newport to everyone in general.

Mick O'Reilly stretched his legs. "No, the opposite, in fact. If you take on one job after another, without any extra pay or whatever, the last thing you get is respect. You're seen as a likeable idiot, a willing workhorse who can be exploited. And it's as simple as that."

"What do you think of the people that Paul and Mick work with, then, Mark?" Helen's grin was mischievous, her tongue a little freer, now that she was more than half way through her second glass of wine.

"They're certainly interesting!"

"Oh, what a diplomat!"

"Delia was a one-off, even by that place's standards, it has to be said. I've never met anyone who got turned on by conflict as much as she did," said Mick.

"From what Paul says, she seemed to be obsessed by the place," said Helen.

"Yes, I'd say that that was the right way to describe her. It was like a drug to her – not the work itself, but all the trouble-making and aggro that could go with it." Another gulp of beer followed. He pointed to his glass. "It's not bad stuff, this, is it? A good job we're walking home tonight, with a police officer here! Anyway, what was I saying? Oh, yes, about Delia... It was Maureen who noticed this, actually..." He broke off and turned to Mark Newport. "That's Maureen Threlfall, who teaches History. She's retiring at the end of this year, which is a shame. She's a great colleague, and a lovely person with it."

"She always seems so nice and incredibly sensible."

"She is, Helen. Anyway, it was Maureen who noticed something strange about Delia whenever the end of term came near. You know how most people, normal people, start to relax as the end of term approaches? Well, with Delia it was the opposite. She used to get jumpy, nervy, even for her."

"What you're saying is, she couldn't live without the place," said Julie Newport, shaking her head.

"How sad," said Helen. She doesn't have any kids, does she – or do they no longer live at home now?"

"No, no kids. She never had any," said Mick.

So nobody knows about her having had children, thought Mark Newport as he helped himself to some crisps.

"So if Maureen's retiring," said Colette as a thought hit her. "who'll take her place on the College Academic Board, then?"

"Oh, didn't I tell you? There was a ballot for it on Friday."

"Who was standing?"

"Dominic Carruthers, Ingrid Kaltz and Veronica Makepeace."

"Delia didn't stand?"

"Well," said Mick, "I suppose she knew deep down that nobody except Liz Goodwin would vote for her. I still can't fathom what there was between Delia and Liz, you know."

So nobody knows about Delia having had children, or about Liz Goodwin having an abortion, thought Mark Newport as he swilled down the remains of his beer.

"I was a bit surprised at Veronica Makepeace standing for the Academic Board, " said Paul. "It was a last minute job, wasn't it?"

"That's right," said Mick. "I thought it strange at the time, as well. And guess who persuaded her to stand? Delia."

"Delia?" said Paul. "Why did she do that?"

"To stop Ingrid from getting all the anti-Dominic votes. Delia hated Ingrid with a passion."

And did Ingrid hate Delia in return, with a passion so great that she could kill her? thought Mark Newport as he gave Paul a smile of thanks on being given another beer.

"It didn't dawn on me why Delia got Veronica to stand," Mick O'Reilly went on, "until I overheard Delia telling Liz about her little scheme. And Veronica, being Veronica, won't have realised that she was merely being used by Delia to get at Ingrid. Stinks, doesn't it?"

"So when the results are out tomorrow, that'll start another little civil war."

"You're probably right, Paul. Good grief, just think – Delia can even cause aggro when she's dead." He held up a hand. "Oh, I shouldn't have said that, but you know what I mean." He looked across at Mark Newport and gave a sad smile. "God knows what you must be thinking!"

"Well, I suppose there are politics and intrigue in every job."

Another diplomatic answer, thought Julie, as she gave her husband a quick grin.

"And according to Maureen, Harold Cassidy's retiring next year," said Mick. At the questioning looks, he added, "His wife let it out at some do, after she'd had a few too many. Maureen and her husband met the Cassidys by chance at some wedding a few weeks ago. Maureen told me today."

"That'll be interesting," said Paul. "So they'll be advertising for a new Head of Department."

"Which Fisher will be after, probably."

"What, that sciver!" said Colette. "It'll be worse than it is with Cassidy! He has no chance, surely?"

"He has a very good chance, when you think he plays golf with the Chairman of the Board of Governors and has a few contacts with Church people."

"I just haven't got that sort of money! You know I haven't!" Rosemary Hepworth stared at the wall as her wet hand grasped the telephone. "But I can't even afford that much! I'm paying all I can afford as it is!"

The voice at the other end was cold, implacable.

"But if my husband found out… You know what that would do to us, my husband, the children. Please stop it, please leave me alone. I've got to go, he's coming upstairs."

She switched her mobile off just before her husband came into the bedroom and abruptly turned her face away.

"Who were you talking to? Susan Barrow again?"

She faced the mirror on the wall, hoping he wouldn't notice her distress in the dim light of the room.

"Oh, it was Veronica, Veronica Makepeace. She wanted to know if I had done some typing for her today, that was all."

Colin Hepworth shook his head. "Good heavens, can't they leave you alone in that place? Do they have to phone you at home in the evening? Why can't you be given an assistant, if there's so much typing to be done?"

She pretended to fix her hair, her face riveted on the mirror, tears still in her eyes. "Well, never mind, it doesn't matter."

"It does matter. You weren't feeling too well a month or so ago. I'm sure that was through overwork and stress. You look pale now." He looked at his watch. "Anyway, are you ready? Come on, we'll be late for the first round of the quiz. Everyone will be wondering where we are."

I'm going to tell him what's happening, first thing tomorrow morning when I get into work, she thought as she followed her husband down the stairs. *It involves him as well as it involves me.*

"You know I mentioned those two prats at St Barnabas's University College who ended up not speaking to each other?"

"You taught there years ago, as well, didn't you, Mick?"

"That's right, Paul." He emptied his pint glass. "By God, it's good stuff, this. Anyway, what was I saying?"

"You're out of your head," said his wife.

"No I'm not. Anyway… yes, St Barnabas's. They invited me back there to give a talk on anti-war literature. And it was most interesting."

"In what way, Mick?" Paul spilt some beer on the carpet, his wife shaking her head.

"Well, when I worked there years before, there was a gang like Cassidy, Fisher and Bent, and another gang of arse-lickers who sucked up to them. But this is the interesting thing," he said, winking at Paul as he passed him another can, "when I went back to give that talk, those little shits who had been half way up the arses of those above them had by then got promotion themselves..."

"And they in turn had a new group sucking up to them," said Paul.

"Exactly. And so it goes on."

"A bit like living in a developing country, I suppose," said Colette. "The people living there know it's corrupt, but can't do anything about it because the next generation of so-called leaders who come along are just as corrupt."

"Precisely. And that was another thing that happened today," said Mick, looking across the room to Paul, burping on the last syllable of the sentence. "I was coming out of the main building when I saw that bloody Wendover woman hit a student's car when she was trying to park. No apology, no nothing. I went across to see if everything was all right. Then Lucy Wendover started telling me to mind my own business."

"Who was the student, Mick?"

"Liz Farne, third year."

"Oh, yes, a good student, a really nice girl. A big Lincoln City fan." He grinned on seeing his wife roll her eyes at Julie Newport and shake her head. "Anyway, how did Liz take it?"

"Oh, OK, in the end. There was no damage done – but it was the woman's snotty attitude that got to me, and to Liz."

"Who's Lucy Wendover, then?"

"Oh, the P.A. of one of the management lot. I must have mentioned her to you. A right snotty cow."

"Wendover?" said Julie Newport thoughtfully. "That's an unusual name – almost as unusual as Newport," she added, digging her husband. "It must be the same one."

"The same one as who?" asked Mick.

"The grandmother of one of the kids I taught in year one was called Wendover, and I think her first name was Lucy. A horrible woman. She sometimes picked the kid up after school. I remember her because of how nasty she was over one particular incident. Her grandchild had picked up a ruler and, for no reason, hit another child across the face with it, cutting his cheek. The child's parents were furious, and rightly so. And you know what? The next day, I got a letter from the Wendover woman telling me that it was the school's fault for allowing rulers to be within the reach of the children, and that she had a good mind to take the matter further with the Governors because of, wait for it, the trauma *her* grandchild had suffered. There was no sense of shame, nothing. If that had been me, I'd have crawled under a stone with embarrassment."

"That's right," said Mick, "but, you see, her little darling grandchild wasn't to blame, the school was! It's always someone else's fault! The blame culture gone mad!"

"The family's not from here. The kid kept telling me that his family were all from the Lake District somewhere. Pity they hadn't stayed there!" Julie Newport then turned to her husband, her tongue loosened a little by her three glasses of wine. "You've been very quiet, Detective Sergeant. I bet you've made notes on all of this, haven't you?"

Mick laughed. "They'll be bloody interesting ones! They're bound to be, about that place!" He turned to the policeman. "Have you met any of our esteemed managers yet?"

Mark Newport grinned. "Only someone called Bent."

Both Mick and Paul burst out laughing. "Oh, God, he's a right pillock! If ever anyone takes himself seriously, it's him, with his clipboards and paper pushing!" Mick O'Reilly's tone suddenly became serious. "He's typical of the business mentality types who've taken over in education. They see it purely as a business, they have no sympathy with what education is supposed to be about. They couldn't give a toss about the welfare of the staff, and still less about the students."

"You can tell that from the language they use," said Paul. "I remember a meeting a few weeks ago, when Harold Cassidy said 'We must sell the individuality of our product'. I sat there thinking, is this a college I'm working in, or a department store?"

"Exactly," said Mick. "To these people, there's no difference. And this mentality has been passed down to the students and their parents. That's why you have young people coming in, with one-tenth of your experience and qualifications, complaining about the mark you've given them, telling you the mark they think they should have got."

"Yes, but they aren't students these days, are they?" said Colette. "They're 'customers'. And, as they are 'customers', they'll complain if they feel let down. I mean, if you're a customer in some department store and you buy a telly there, you go back and complain if it turns out not to be as good as you'd thought, don't you? Well, if you're a 'customer' as a student and you get a mark that turns out to be not as good as you'd thought, then in the very same way you go and complain about the 'quality' of that mark to the person that you got it from."

"That's right," said Helen. "If you accept the ridiculous idea that education is a business just like any other, then that's what's going to happen. And it's going to happen more and more with people having to pay towards tuition fees – now they see themselves as 'buying' a degree."

"And it's people like Bent who've hijacked education for their own ends," said Mick. "And when you think of the life he leads!"

"In what way?" asked Helen.

"Well, he came to Parkdale as a promotion, from some college in London. But his wife and family didn't want to come here. His kids are missing all their friends, they don't like their new school, his wife has found it hard to settle here. They've had all sorts of problems."

"All because of his promotion."

Mick nodded. "That's right, Helen. What sort of life is that, for God's sake? And what for? Just so he can have a special plaque on his office door and go strutting around like an idiot? Ridiculous."

A few minutes later, Julie Newport looked at her watch and turned to her husband. "Time we went, Mark. Poor Linda will think we're never coming back."

"Is that your baby-sitter, Julie?" asked Colette.

"Yes."

"They were the days! Are you planning on returning to teaching when the children are a bit older?"

"Yes, more than likely. How long have you been in teaching?"

Colette O'Reilly laughed. "More years than I care to remember, Julie!" She made a rapid calculation in her head. "Nearly thirty years now. I'm going part-time next year, though. I've had enough, really. What with the paperwork that's invented all the time, nonsense like Ofsted, certain parents who know their rights and are down on you like a ton of bricks at the slightest thing... Don't let me put you off, Julie! But I've had enough." She shook her head. "The job bears little resemblance to the job I went into all those years ago."

Chapter 11

Ray Farrar had spent a restless evening. Even when he had tried to take his mind off the case by watching the football, he kept thinking about certain things that people had said, certain things that didn't seem to fit, certain things that tantalisingly hinted at some sort of link or connection. On two occasions his wife, much to her annoyance, had spoken to him without getting a reply, even during the half-time break.

As usual, he had discussed the case with her, and she was convinced that the fact that two people connected to the College had been murdered in such a short space of time was no coincidence. She also thought that the former student who had been seen on the campus and in the town could well be central to the whole case.

Neither did sleep come easily. He lay awake in the soft darkness of a warm night, tossing and turning, passing things through his mind time and time again. Had Delia Bumstead really lost two children? Not just *one*, but *two*... That seemed a remarkable tragedy, if it was true... And yet her husband, the enigmatic Barry Bumstead, had flatly denied that she'd had children. Was that because, as Gillian Taylor had suggested, it had been so awful an experience that he had blocked it out of his mind? Or had Delia Bumstead been talking figuratively? Or had she given birth to two children *before* she met her husband, and he knew nothing of it? That was the trouble with these arty-farty types, you never knew what level they were operating on... No, that's not right, we know for an established fact that at some time in her life she had given birth to at least one child. Perhaps she *had* given birth, but they had been stillborn? Or had they been twins, and she'd had them adopted? That would be quite easy to trace, either under her maiden name or married name...

And why had Valerie Salter wanted to speak with Dominic Carruthers and then fail to turn up? Was he telling the whole truth, or were there elements in his story that were somewhat selective? And why had the woman called Barrow disappeared? Had she just flipped, or was there something more to it than that...?

"For goodness sake, go to sleep. It's almost two o'clock in the morning."

"All right, Andrea, sorry..."

Then there was the thing that Gillian had overheard in the office about Delia

Bumstead refusing to teach a group because Terry Trotter would have been somehow involved... Was there anything in that, or was it just malicious gossip? And the secretary, Rosemary Hepworth, was hiding something, she just seemed paranoid all the time... What were she and the nurse talking about when he'd overheard part of their conversation? All the different characters that worked there: the vague Head of Department, the articulate sciver who was his assistant, the nutcases who wanted to bring revolution (as long as they had their big houses and posh cars), that funny Belgian bloke, the calm efficient Ingrid woman. Was she *too* calm, too much in control? Then there was that self-important prat called Bent... that cocky student with his student union aspirations... The student, yes... The strange thing about this case was that the murder of someone else, a former student quite far away in Manchester, had cast just as long a shadow as Delia Bumstead's murder... Andrea's right, find the girl called Salter, that's a priority...

I'll write him a quick note about last night's phone call and stick it under the door of his office, thought Rosemary Hepworth as she drove into the college car park. Ten minutes or so later, she came into the office to find Mick O'Reilly already there, standing in front of his pigeon-hole.

"What's this?"

Mick O'Reilly was always one of the first staff to arrive each day, and this morning was no exception. He stared at the sheet of paper that he held in his hand.

"All staff have got one, Mick," she said as she brushed past him on her way to her desk. "Lucy Wendover brought them over in an envelope."

Mick O'Reilly read the memo for a second time.

Memo to all staff

Extremely Important

A meeting is to take place at 11.00 today to discuss the possibility of a merger between the Department of Social and Language Studies and the Department of Business Studies. It is imperative that all staff attend.

Cuthbert Bent, Assistant Director (Personnel).

"I haven't heard anything about this."

"No, you won't have, Mick." The secretary spoke as though correcting a naughty child. He looked across at her.

"Does this mean that *you* have known about it?"

She ran a hand through her hair. "Certain staff have been privy to this development, yes."

"Privy? And how long has this so-called development been going on?"

"For about the last two months."

"What! And only *certain* staff? And who are categorised as *certain* staff?"

"The Director and his Assistants, Heads of Department and administrative staff."

He stared at her. "You mean to tell me that the teaching staff are completely in the dark about something as important as this?"

"Well, it was felt that this is such an important matter that it was thought it wouldn't be appropriate for the teaching staff to know."

He roared with laughter. "It was felt by whom? And the teaching staff are less important than office staff, are they?" He lowered his head in mock apology. "Oh, sorry, did I say office *staff*? I meant office *managers*, of course. The whole bloody country is run by *managers* these days, isn't it, whole battalions of them, thousands of them."

Terry Trotter and Jean-Luc Lafarge were coming into the office just as Mick O'Reilly was going out. "There's a nice little surprise for you in your pigeon-hole, Terry, Jean-Luc," he said.

He had only gone a few yards away from the office when he heard an enraged bellow from Terry Trotter and a cry of "They are taking the shit!" from the Belgian.

"And the Head of Department's retiring next year, with Fisher, the Assistant Head, fancying his chances of taking over," said Mark Newport, bringing to a close his account of the evening spent at the Richardsons' house.

"Well done, Mark," said Ray Farrar. "You managed to pick up some very interesting snippets of information last night." He sat back in his chair and looked at all of his colleagues. "So it would seem that no-one on the staff knows about Delia Bumstead having had a child, or children, then, and no-one knows about what drew her and Liz Goodwin together." He was about to say something else when there was a knock on the door.

At his call, the door opened and a thin woman with a pale face and medium length dark hair showing wisps of grey appeared. Her brown eyes had a direct stare.

"Good morning," she said. "I have come to apologise for my absence yesterday. My name is Susan Barrow."

Ray Farrar got up from his chair. "I see. Good morning, Miss Barrow." He briefly introduced his colleagues, then invited her to sit down. "As we are all here, perhaps you could tell us why you weren't available yesterday and where you were."

She held her arms out wide and then clasped her hands. "I… I couldn't help it. Things get on top of me at times. Have you heard of GAD?" She pronounced the letters separately. "General Anxiety Disorder. You worry about everything and nothing. I know it's stupid, I know it's irrational, but there you are. It's the way I'm made – or it's the way I've become, at least."

Gillian Taylor shifted in her chair. She had a neighbour with the same condition, a woman who would suddenly call her around midnight and give her a list of worries, most of them trivial in themselves, that were gnawing away at her.

"And do you have medication for this, Miss Barrow?"

"Yes, but it only controls it. It can't cure it." She scratched at her arm. "And working in a place like this isn't exactly helpful, either, not with the way some people behave."

"Some people?"

She looked flustered yet somehow defiant at the same time. "Well, Delia Bumstead for one."

"I see." The inspector thought for a few seconds before continuing. "We are led to believe that Delia Bumstead was directly responsible for you not being appointed as external examiner at another institution, Miss Barrow. Is that right?"

The woman's hand went to her face as though attempting to hide the sudden blush. "Yes, that's right."

"When did you find out about this?"

"On Friday afternoon." She blush had disappeared, but the eyes remained fearful, haunted.

"And what did you do?"

"I went looking for Delia, but she'd already left for home."

"And did you manage to see her about it before she was killed?"

She played with a ring on the small finger of her left hand. "Did I go to her office and kill her in a fit of rage, you mean? No, I didn't. But I felt like doing it on Friday afternoon, I'm telling you."

She said the last sentence slowly and quietly, nodding her head, her eyes fixed on the inspector's.

"I see," said the inspector, looking at her thoughtfully. It was clear that this was a person whose mind lived on the edge, whose mental state was highly delicate. "As you can appreciate, there are certain questions that we have had to ask all your colleagues. The main one is, can you tell us where you were yesterday morning, say between half eight and half nine?"

She gave a rueful smile. "Firstly, I was at the doctor's. And then I was here, actually, inspector. I'm not going to deny it. I came in, went to my office, tried to sort a few things out, then after the meeting that you called, I felt I couldn't face the day. So I left a note for Rosemary, the secretary, and drove up to Yorkshire, where I stayed the night at a small hotel."

"I see. Miss Barrow, could you tell us how you got on with Dr Bumstead generally, on a day to day basis?"

Another rueful smile followed. "I didn't get on with her, it's as simple as that. Almost nobody did. She was a person who seemed to take delight in rubbing people up the wrong way, in upsetting people. She enjoyed making you feel permanently incapable, incompetent."

"You said before, Miss Barrow," said Gillian Taylor, "or certainly implied, that there are other people besides Delia Bumstead that you have had difficulties with. Who are they, and what were the difficulties over?"

She shrugged her shoulders almost like a child. "Well, various people on the staff, sometimes students. About all sorts of things, things that crop up in any working situation from day to day."

"I see. Thank you." *What aren't you telling us?* she wondered as she sat back in her chair.

A few minutes later, Ray Farrar brought the interview to a close. He thanked the woman for coming to see them, asking her also to stay on the campus in case she was needed for more questions.

Gillian Taylor and Alan Henry went off to the student health centre to chat with nurse Richmond. Her conversation with Rosemary Hepworth that had been partially overheard by their boss seemed highly interesting.

Seconds later, there was a little tap at the door, and Ray Farrar opened it. He could tell by the woman's face that she had something interesting to tell. He tried to remain calm as he spoke to her.

"Good morning, Mrs McAteer."

"I see the democratic process is alive and kicking, then, Mick," said Maureen Threlfall as she shot a sardonic glance at the typed sheet pinned to the centre of the staff notice board.

"Well, well, surprise, surprise. The vote was split in Dominic's favour, eh? So poor Ingrid was robbed."

Maureen gave a grim smile. "Incredible, isn't it? Delia's actually managed to get at Ingrid even after her own death. Is there anything that woman wasn't capable of?"

Mick did a rapid calculation. "Dominic got seven votes, Ingrid five, and four going to Veronica." He nodded his head knowingly. "Yes, so if it had been a straight fight between Ingrid and Dominic, the chances are she would have won it. Let's see, you, me, Paul and Frances will have voted for Ingrid, along with Ingrid herself of course."

"And Veronica got three votes," said Maureen. "That would be Veronica herself, Harriet of course, and someone else... Jean-Luc, perhaps."

"No, I did not vote for her," he cut in from behind. "I voted for Dominic, if you must know. And why? Well, I could not vote for Ingrid. She is forcing me to work unsocialist hours. I told Dominic. He is kind - he said that if he was elected, he would support me."

"And do you believe him, Jean-Luc?"

"Yes. And by voting for him and not voting for Ingrid, I was able to kill the one bird with two stones."

"Do you also believe in Father Christmas, as well, Jean-Luc?" asked Maureen.

"Dominic is all right! With him on the Hacademic Board, it will be a whole new balls game!" the Belgian shouted. "He always says we are all equal, you have heard him yourself!"

"Oh yes, Dominic *says* we are all equal, Jean-Luc…"

"And he believes it!"

"No, Jean-Luc. What Dominic and people like him believe is that we are all *equally inferior* to *him*."

The Belgian spread out his hands and hunched his shoulders. "OK, so Dominic is ambitious…"

"And therefore not to be trusted." Thinking that she might have sounded patronising to her colleague, Maureen added, "Is next week's open day for sixth formers still on, Jean-Luc, do you know?"

He shrugged his shoulders. "Yes, I think so… yes, the list of students who are going to help showing them around is here."

"Well," said Harriet Bond, who had suddenly appeared, "I only hope we get the right calibre of student showing them around."

Mick O'Reilly grinned. "What do you mean, Harriet?"

She pointed to the list. "Well, look at Anne Dickinson, for instance – and Liam Draper. They aren't exactly masters of the Queen's English, are they?"

Mick's grin became even bigger. "You mean, you can tell by the way they speak that they aren't from a middle class background, Harriet? A bit like me?"

The woman reddened. "Oh, you know what I mean…"

"Speaking as a foreigner from north of the border," said Maureen, exaggerating each "r" in "border", "why is it that you English are obsessed with the way people speak? Why is it that, in England, the most important thing about a person isn't how nice they are, or how genuine they are, but how they sound when they open their mouth?"

Harriet Bond shaped her mouth as though to say something, then stormed out of the office instead.

Gillian Taylor and Alan Henry were walking past Eric Fisher's office on the way to speak to nurse Richmond when they heard voices from inside. The door hadn't been properly closed. They instinctively stopped and listened. The Assistant Head of Department was talking to Dominic Carruthers.

"Well, congratulations on being elected to the Academic Board, Dominic. This place needs people with a sense of responsibility and morality in the management structure."

"Oh, thank you, Eric. I can only say I feel privileged to have been elected. I'll do my best, of course, to represent the interests of the department and its staff."

"I would have stood myself, of course, but I'm just so busy all the time. You can imagine, of course, Dominic. I sometimes think I must be mad, when I think of the hours I spend here."

"Oh, I can well believe it, Eric. I suppose people just don't realise the workload that you and Harold get through, all the hassle and flak you have to face, the interminable meetings…"

"Absolutely. I do think that Harold has made the right decision to retire next year."

"Er, speaking of which, Eric, four walls and all that, of course… I can think of no better solution to that problem than you being appointed as his successor…"

A short modest laugh followed.

"Get me a bucket, I'm going to puke," whispered Gillian Taylor.

Alan Henry shook his head sadly. "It'll need to be a big bucket. I might be joining you."

"Oh, I can say most sincerely that I've never ever harboured ambitions of that nature, Dominic… Do you think I'd have a chance?"

"Oh, good grief, yes, Eric. You're highly qualified, you're highly experienced in administration. It's a natural progression, surely…"

"Well, all that might change, of course, with the proposed merger with Business Studies that's going to be discussed this morning."

"Yes, but Ted Crapper is retiring at the end of next year, isn't he? And Cuthbert Bent was saying to me at a Rotary dinner last weekend that he can't see anyone ready to fit into a Head of Department's shoes in the Business Studies department. OK, there's Jack Bannister – but he's only got an MA, a PhD, written a couple of books and been external examiner at half a dozen other institutions."

"Mm. He'd be too academic, you mean?"

"Good God, yes! We don't want academics to have a say in things! The place would go to rack and ruin!"

"We need managers…"

"Exactly, Eric. And there aren't enough of them these days, that's the trouble with this country."

"So what you're saying is…"

"What I'm saying is, Eric, you're the perfect man to be the Head of a new combined department called, say, Business and Social Studies…"

"Yes… I can see where you're coming from, Dominic…"

And I can see where you want to be going to, as well, Dominic – into his shoes as next Assistant Head of the new department, you slimy little shit, thought Gillian Taylor. Glancing at Alan Henry, she could see that he was thinking the same.

"It would make perfect sense to me, Eric."

"Yes, the problem is, Dominic, getting others to share your view… Another problem is that there could well be others in the department who see themselves as a possible Head."

"No, no, Eric. Who? There's Mick O'Reilly, and what does he do? All he ever does is worry about the students. Ridiculous!"

"True, true…"

"And the only other possible candidate would be Terry Trotter – OK, he's improved the number of students doing French, but so what?"

"Well, what have students got to do with it!"

"Precisely!"

"So you're quite optimistic of favourable developments in the near future, then, Dominic?"

"Oh, yes, Eric. I have the ear of the Archdeacon of Parkdale, you know, and this is still technically a Church institution… and I play badminton with a few other governors. I'm also godfather to Cuthbert Bent's grandson…"

"Really? Excellent, excellent. Fine, Dominic…"

"Er, look, perhaps you and your wife would like to come to dinner on Friday evening, Eric?"

"That would be very nice, Dominic. Very nice indeed. And, er, perhaps it would give us an opportunity to discuss this a little bit further. I'm very grateful for your support. This won't be forgotten."

"Oh, it's a pleasure, Eric. Think nothing of it. Friday, then. Let's say about eight."

As they heard footsteps come towards the door, the two police officers immediately stepped away and stood on the other side of the corridor. The door opened and Dominic Carruthers came out just as Lucinda Hobbs-Smithers and Jean-Luc Lafarge were coming out of Rosemary Hepworth's office.

"Hi, guys," said Dominic Carruthers. He casually jerked a thumb in the direction of Eric Fisher's office. "I've just been in there, with Fisher. I've told him a few home truths, I'm telling you."

"Ooh, Dominic, what did you say to him?"

"I told him he was a tosser, Lucinda, a complete and utter tosser, a bloody waste of space who should be ashamed of himself."

"That's so brave of you, Dominic!"

Jean-Luc beamed in admiration. "So you took him to the dry cleaners! Excellent, mon brave!"

Dominic Carruthers smiled modestly. "Well, there are times in life when you've just got to make a moral stand, aren't there?"

Just then one of the cleaners appeared from a small room that the cleaners and porters shared together. Alf Jones was a small, wiry man with grey hair, nervous and eager to please. When Dominic Carruthers saw him, he snapped his fingers at him and beckoned him to come to him.

"Did you clean my office this morning?"

"Yes, sir, I did, sir."

"Well you didn't clean it very well, did you? There was still one piece of sweet paper in the rubbish bin next to my desk."

The man looked terrified and seemed to make himself even smaller. "Oh, I'm sorry, sir-"

"Don't let it happen again, do you hear?"

"No, I won't sir. I'm sorry, sir. It's my wife, you see, she's not been too well recently."

"I said, don't let it happen again. Or I'll have to report you for negligence. Do I make myself understood?"

He then ushered Alf Jones away with a sweep of his hand before turning to Lucinda Hobbs-Smithers. "I'll see you at the talk I'm giving tonight, then, Lucinda."

"Absolutely, Dominic. What's the title again?"

"Its title is *Why I'm a Marxist: All people are equal.*"

Ray Farrar and Mark Newport stared at the woman intently. The inspector edged his body towards her as he spoke.

"Please say that again, Mrs McAteer. You're saying that the student you contacted last night definitely said that Valerie Salter was expecting Michael Springer's baby and that he forced her to have an abortion?"

She swallowed, then nodded her head slowly. "Yes, that's right. That's what made Kevin fall out with him. Kevin's a very devout Catholic, you see, and has very strong feelings about such things... Strangely enough, Valerie was from a Catholic family as well. I don't know whether or not they ever knew about her having an abortion..."

"Well, we're grateful to you for telling us all this, Mrs McAteer. Every bit of information is useful."

She sighed, sadly and listlessly. "I just thought, well, I just thought you should know, I don't know why... It's just that, with Michael being murdered recently, it might have something to do with it all..." She raised her eyes to the ceiling. "Oh, I don't know, I'm sorry I've told you now. I wish Maureen had advised me not to say anything ..."

Ray Farrar shook his head vigorously. "No, no, Mrs McAteer, you've done the right thing. You never know, you may have pinpointed another line of enquiry for us into Michael Springer's death." He leaned forward again. "And you have my word that what you have told us will be treated as totally confidential."

The woman smiled nervously as she left the room, Mark Newport closing it securely behind her before turning around.

"An interesting little piece of information, sir."

"Yes, Mark, too right it is." Ray Farrar got up and stared at the light rain hitting the window.

"So we contact Valerie Salter, then sir? The College must have her home address."

"I've tried that already, Mark. She didn't live too far from here."

Mark Newport studied his superior. "Go on, sir…"

"Her parents were both killed in a car accident two months ago. The secretary told me – it had been in the local press."

"What? Oh no. So there's no-one to contact except the girl herself, then?"

"So it would seem, Mark. But there's something else interesting, as well. We'll see what Gillian and Alan say about it when they come back from seeing nurse Richmond."

"What's that, sir?"

"I've done some checking of dates. Valerie Salter's letter to Delia Bumstead, asking if she could see her, was written only a week after her parents had been killed." The rain mesmerised him again. "Now why would she want to do that?"

"No, Dr O'Reilly, it *is not* a fait accompli!"

One of the many things about Cuthbert Bent that fascinated Mick O'Reilly was that whenever he got annoyed, his nose would become crimson, a phenomenon which gave credence to the widespread view that the Assistant Director (Personnel) and Highland malts were more than just good friends.

"Then why have staff been kept in the dark about this proposed merger?"

"Staff have not been kept in the dark," said Lucy Wendover, looking up from the notes that she was taking, from which the minutes of the meeting would be produced and circulated.

"With respect, Mrs Wendover, I was speaking to the Assistant Director, not to you. You're only here to take the minutes."

Cuthbert Bent's secretary set her crimson mouth in a thin line as she glared at Mick O'Reilly for a few seconds.

"As Lucy has just stated, staff have not been kept in the dark. We are discussing it with staff now!" said Cuthbert Bent, his voice rising a little.

"Yes," continued Mick, "but only when planning is at an advanced stage. Why weren't the views of staff taken into account much earlier?"

"Because it wasn't thought necessary!"

"By whom, and on what grounds?" asked Maureen Threlfall.

"By the College's management, Mrs Throughfall."

"Then can you tell us why it is that the secretarial staff knew about it all when the teaching staff didn't?"

Bernie Bent squinted at Maureen Threlfall from over his glasses, his little eyes becoming even tinier. "By secretarial staff, I assume you mean administrative staff. Hm? The administrative staff play a major role in the life of this institution."

"So do the teaching staff," said Frances McAteer.

The eyes became the size of pin heads. "What? Do you not realise that without the administrative staff, these important people, this College would not exist?"

"Ah well, as long as we know where we stand, then," said Mick O'Reilly with a sardonic grin. "People doing administrative work are seen as being more important than those who do unimportant things like teaching."

"Precisely."

Ray Farrar, sitting to one side of the room, could see Rosemary Hepworth preen herself for a few seconds.

"And will this *proposed* merger," said Ingrid Kaltz, dwelling on the adjective, "mean that the content of some of our academic work will be changed?"

Cuthbert Bent shifted in his seat. "There will, perforce, be certain modifications that will have to take place, yes."

There was a chorus of shouting, which gradually subsided as Terry Trotter stood up. "And what form will these so-called modifications take?"

The Assistant Director (Personnel) cleared his throat. "It has to be pointed out to you all that this College has to move with the times…"

"Ah," said Terry Trotter, "you mean that instead of teaching arts-based subjects such as literature and history, we'll be having to teach stuff to do with business?"

"If you put it like that, well, yes. Teaching will have to be slanted towards the world of business and commerce." He silenced the groans of disapproval with a wave of his hand. "For instance, the sociology syllabus could be changed to include things like the way the different social classes purchase things in department stores…"

"Or Maureen could teach special History modules on the rise of the Co-op," said Mick while nudging Paul Richardson.

"Exactly, Dr O'Reilly, exactly!" The tiny eyes gleamed. "I knew you'd see sense! There are all sorts of opportunities for those who have the vision, the creativity! Seize the moment! Carpe die!"

"Or even diem."

"Exactly, that as well, Dr O'Reilly."

"Yes," said Ingrid Kaltz, gently kicking Mick's foot under the table. "Perhaps we could have a history module on the art of the Renaissance, but not studying the works of Giotto or Michelangelo for their artistic beauty and spiritual meaningfulness, but from the point of view of how much money you could get for them if they were sold."

Cuthbert Bent clapped his hands together rapturously. "Yes! Yes! Exactly! As you can all see, the possibilities for the new Department of Business are endless!"

He put his hand to his mouth as he realised what he had just said.

"Ah!" shouted Jean-Luc. "So this is all an over-take by the Business School! We are wasting our time discussing all this. It is spanking a dead horse!"

"Er, you don't spank a dead horse, Mr Lafarge," said Cuthbert Bent, grinning.

Jean-Luc tapped his forefinger against his nose and smiled knowingly. "What I do in my own house is my business!"

"Anyway," said Cuthbert Bent, gathering up his papers in an obvious sign that, as far as he was concerned, the meeting was approaching its end, "I would advise you all to think long and hard about modifying your teaching areas to the world of business." He turned to Harold Cassidy, who had sat silently throughout. "In the meantime, Harold, we'll have to do an in-depth study of the new structures that will come into force. There'll be a management team, deputy managers, assistant managers..."

"Not to mention deputy assistant managers, assistant deputy managers, assistant deputy under-managers..." said Mick.

"Exactly," said Cuthbert Bent, his head nodding vigorously. "It's good to see that some people are learning sense at last and getting their priorities right."

"And in the meantime, what is being done about staff shortages?" asked Maureen Threlfall.

"Nothing is being done, Mrs Throughfall. And nothing is being done because nothing can be done. There isn't the money." He leaned forward across the desk. "Have you any idea how much it has cost to lay new carpets in all the management offices? These things don't come free, you know."

"That's very true, Maureen," said Mick with a straight face. "It's all very well for you to complain about the state the lecture rooms are in. That's only about teaching and students."

"Exactly," said Cuthbert Bent. "That's precisely what the Principal was saying to me yesterday afternoon when he phoned me from Antigua."

"Antigua?" said Ingrid Kaltz. "What in heaven's name is he doing there? I thought you said there was no money available?"

The Assistant Director gave her a patronising smile. "The Principal's trip is from another financial source, earmarked for research trips."

"Freebies, you mean."

The man became incandescent. "And what is that supposed to mean? The Principal is engaged on very important research on inter-disciplinary management processes."

"But I thought he was at a conference in Birmingham doing that," said Frances McAteer.

"That was the original plan, yes. But then the Antigua option suddenly appeared," said Lucy Wendover from above her glasses.

"So the Principal thought that he would study these processes in Antigua rather than Birmingham," said Frances.

"For strictly educational and professional reasons, of course, Frances," said Mick.

At that moment there was a knock at the door, and one of the receptionists from the main building appeared.

"Yes, Kerry, what is it?" asked Cuthbert Bent.

"I'm sorry to interrupt, Mr Bent, but I have a message for Mrs Threlfall."

"What is it?" asked Maureen.

"I'm afraid I have a bit of bad news, Mrs Threlfall. Your husband's just phoned to say that your mother's had a heart attack and is in intensive care."

Maureen put her hand to her mouth and rushed out of the room, Mick and Frances following her.

"Maureen," he shouted as she raced down the corridor towards the car park, "let us know if we can do anything."

He returned to the room to find Lucinda Hobbs-Smithers trying to attract Cuthbert Bent's attention by waving her arm in the air.

"Yes, Lucinda," he said, inviting her to speak.

"I wish to register a formal complaint, Cuthbert. I think it's most unprofessional to have our important business interrupted by someone's family problems."

"Yes, I agree, Lucinda," said Lucy Wendover. "Cuthbert and I will look into it."

"I wonder what they were like," murmured Mick to Paul Richardson, nodding his head in the direction of Lucinda Hobbs-Smithers as he sat down.

"Who?"

"Her parents."

Chapter 12

"Nurse Richmond, please don't feel in any way guilty about what you've just told us." Gillian Taylor looked at the woman earnestly. "You have our solemn promise that the information you have given us will be dealt with in the strictest confidence, and will only be used if it has any connection with either the murder we are investigating at the moment or with Michael Springer's murder."

She looked at her colleague for confirmation, and Alan Henry met the nurse's eyes and nodded.

"It's something that's been on my mind since Michael was murdered." The woman's voice had become no more than a whisper. "It might have nothing to do with it, of course, nothing at all…"

"You may well be right, nurse Richmond," said Alan Henry. "In which case, there's no harm done. What you have told us will be treated as just a piece of personal information on someone which has no relevance to the case."

"And we give you our word that nothing, not a single thing, of this conversation will be divulged to the press," said Gillian Taylor. "Obviously, of course, we're going to inform Inspector Farrar of what you have told us. We have to, obviously. But rest assured that everything will be treated most discreetly. You have our word on that."

"If, in the meantime, you find out how we can contact Valerie Salter, we would be most grateful, nurse Richmond," added Alan Henry as he got up from his chair.

A few minutes later, they were waiting outside the room where Ray Farrar and Mark Newport had been attending the meeting chaired by Cuthbert Bent. As soon as the inspector saw them, he knew they had something to tell.

"Well, what is it, then?" he asked as soon as they went out of the building.

"Well, first of all, sir, we found out from the nurse that Valerie Salter had an abortion a few years ago, when she was a student here."

"Go on." He tried to look impassively at Gillian Taylor, not wanting to dampen her enthusiasm by telling her that he and Mark had found that out already from Frances McAteer.

"The father was Michael Springer, sir…" She stopped, a wry smile on her lips. "You know that already, don't you, sir…"

He smiled grimly and made a vague gesture with his hand. "Only since this morning. Frances McAteer told us. She found out about it herself only last night, through someone else who was in the same year as Valerie Salter and Michael Springer." He looked at her and then at Alan Henry. "But there's something else nurse Richmond's told you, isn't there?"

"Well, sir," said Alan Henry, "she said that when Valerie Salter came to her telling her she was pregnant and that she wanted an abortion, she'd tried to dissuade her from having one – she said that she's a Catholic, and so was Valerie. Then Valerie broke down and said that Michael Springer would dump her if she didn't have the abortion. I expect you know that, as well."

"Yes, we do. But go on."

"Well, she also told nurse Richmond that she couldn't bear to go through with having the baby and then having it adopted because she'd been adopted herself."

"What?" Ray Farrar's throat went dry.

"And according to nurse Richmond, Valerie came back to her later and started asking her for advice on how she could find out who her real parents were."

"Really?" The palms of his hands were now clammy. He suddenly looked at the officer nearest to him. "Alan, I want Valerie Salter's file immediately."

"So why are there difficulties with your thesis, Paul?" said Maureen Threlfall as she pulled up a chair.

The staff common room was quite crowded, so they had decided to take a table out on the patio, despite the threatening rain.

"Well, I don't really know, Maureen. My supervisor just said that the External was having second thoughts about my approach, that was all." He suddenly noticed that Mick's mouth was set in a grim line.

"Come on, Mick, what is it?"

"Well, it sounds a bit like the trouble that I had with my PhD, Paul. When you told me who your External was, I immediately had doubts, but I didn't want to get you worried."

"What do you mean?"

"Well, I know for a fact that he has views on Gerald Manley Hopkins that are quite different from yours. And I also know for a fact that he's an opinionated pillock."

"You say that you had some problems with yours, Mick…"

"Well, my PhD was on an eighteenth century English poet, who had Irish sympathies… And my External happened to be someone who was pro British Empire, and all that…"

"Go on…"

"Well, he failed my thesis, so I had to re-write the bloody thing."

Maureen Threlfall snorted. "Bloody typical. And you had to re-write it, Mick, not because it was academically defective, but only because he didn't agree with your arguments and conclusions."

"Exactly."

"And there was nothing you could do about it, of course."

"Nothing at all. He was a big name in that particular field, so I had no choice but to re-write it, feeling totally and utterly dishonest." He shook his head slowly. "And Colette had to type it all out again, because at the time we couldn't afford to get it done professionally. We'd already spent a small fortune getting the thing typed in the first place."

"And knowing as well that you had to re-write it in a certain way for him to give you a PhD?"

"Exactly, Maureen." He played with his teaspoon before letting it fall with a tinkle onto the table. "Pathetic, isn't it? But what do you do? I know very well that the thesis I 'revised' is nowhere near as good as the original one that I'd written, so I suppose I can live with myself in knowing that I should have got the PhD in the first place." He picked up the spoon again. "And the other annoying thing was the fact that it had cost a small fortune to have the bloody thing bound. We were a bit stretched for money at the time – Colette wasn't working, and the boys were very young. And it all came to nothing because of one person's say-so."

"And you think I'm going to have to go through the same thing?" said Paul, his eyes earnest and fearful.

Mick scanned a menacing mass of clouds slowly covering the sky. "Well, I don't want to be gloom and doom, Paul, and everything might be OK in the end.

I hope I'm wrong, but maybe you going to have to revise some of it."

Ray Farrar gave his colleague a puzzled look when he saw that he had returned empty-handed. "Did you get the file, then, Alan?"

"No, sir."

"Why not?"

"I went to the filing cabinet where the files on past students are kept – you know, the one where the secretary got Michael Springer's file out for us – and it wasn't there. It's missing, sir."

"What? Are you sure?"

"Yes, sir. I got the secretary to check with me, to make double sure, and Valerie Salter's file had gone. We went through all the files, to see if by any chance it had been taken out and then put back in the wrong place. But it isn't there."

"Is there anywhere else in the office where it could have been put," said Mark Newport, "you know, a separate filing cabinet or cupboard for students who had done a different set of modules, or whatever?"

"I asked Rosemary Hepworth the same thing, but she said that all the files to do with past students are put in alphabetical order in the one filing cabinet, no matter what the make-up of their degree was."

Ray Farrar started pacing up and down the room, his arms folded. "Now why would someone want to spirit away Valerie Salter's file? And who?"

"I wonder if Rosemary Hepworth noticed anyone near that particular filing cabinet," said Gillian Taylor.

"I asked her that, as well, and she said that she had no recollection of anyone being there. It's immediately behind her desk, so she would have remembered if she had seen anyone."

"The other problem," said Alan Henry, "is that I suppose she leaves the office from time to time, so it could have been pinched while the office was empty."

"Yes, I suppose so," said Ray Farrar, staring through the window. "But what was in that file that has made someone want to stop us from seeing it?" He started pacing up and down the office again. "So let's say it wasn't an outsider who murdered Dr Bumstead, then…" He made a vague motion with both hands. "Sorry, I'm rambling. Let's get back to Valerie Salter…" He rubbed his hands together. "Right, two things. Gillian, Alan, I want you to get the files on all members of staff in the Department. If anyone starts objecting, refer them to me." He rubbed his chin. "Go through them with a fine toothcomb. I want details on everyone's place of birth, former employment, maiden names – anything that might give us a glimmer of information."

"It shouldn't take all that long, sir. There aren't all that many members of staff, and we've already got Delia Bumstead's file."

"True enough, Gillian. See what you can both find, then we'll meet here to discuss anything that looks interesting." The inspector looked at his watch. "Let's say an hour from now, OK?"

"Perhaps the lad that Frances McAteer spoke to last night might be able to help us, sir."

"Precisely what I was thinking, Mark. Let's get his number from Frances McAteer. Then we can phone him and maybe arrange to see him."

"I know what's going to happen, of course, Lucinda."

Rosemary Hepworth was checking the contents of a floppy disk while at the same time trying to listen to a conversation in hushed tones between Dominic Carruthers and Lucinda Hobbs-Smithers. They were facing the pigeon holes and not each other, which made it difficult for her to pick up all of what they were saying.

"What's that, Dominic?"

"Well, with Harold retiring next year…" The secretary silently cursed a lawnmower cutting the grass outside the office and a student who had come into the office asking her if she knew where Harriet Bond was. "… so it's obvious that it's going to go ahead. What do you think?"

"Oh, I do, too. This morning's meeting was just a kite-flying exercise… Cuthbert Bent must know…"

Dominic Carruthers then said something that Rosemary Hepworth couldn't hear. It was enough to make Lucinda Hobbs-Smithers turn to him in surprise.

"Do you think so, Dominic? God, that would be dreadful... even worse than having Harold Cassidy as Head of Department. Is there any way it could be prevented?"

He shook his head vigorously. "No. I know he's a tosser, but he has too many friends in high places, Lucinda. And you know how this place works. I suppose the College would see it as a logical progression to go from Assistant Head of Department to Head of Department..."

"Even though he's only been here a short while?"

Another nod of the head. "Oh, yes, I'm sure of it." His head went towards hers. "There'd be one way of counteracting it, though, Lucinda, though I'd have to have people's support..."

"Go on." She in turn tilted her head towards his as he whispered in her ear. "Good grief, yes! Of course! Yes! You'd make a marvellous Assistant Head of Department, Dominic!..."

"I've been looking at College regulations..." The lawnmower returned. "So that's all that would be needed..."

"Really? Only three?"

"Yes."

"Well, you'd get three members of staff to support you easily."

"Do you think so?"

"Oh, yes, without a doubt. That would really strengthen your application."

"Yes, maybe you're right."

"Oh, I'm convinced of it. Obviously, I'd support you, Jean-Luc could be talked over... and someone like Susan would support it..."

"... if I hinted to her that her teaching load could be lightened for some undemanding admin job..."

"Exactly..."

"I'm only doing it for the sake of the Department, of course... Something's got to be done to put the rein on Eric Fisher's ambitions..."

Then they slowly walked out of the office, leaving her behind her PC. She sat and stared into space for a few moments. *What am I doing here?* she thought. *It's on the brink of ruining my marriage and destroying my family... Why did I ever apply for this damn job...Look at those two who've just gone out. Lies, deceit, pretence, scheming... Is that what life is about? Deceit... just like what I've done to my husband and family...*

She went across to the water-cooler, then returned to her desk and morosely placed the plastic cup on it as she started to examine the contents of the disk. A sudden patter of rain against the window made her look out at the campus and beyond it to the distant hills capped by cloud. She turned her portable radio's volume a little higher. She liked to have *Radio Parkdale* on as background noise while she did the more mechanical aspects of her work.

The jingle told her it was time for the latest news bulletin. When she heard the first item of news, the shock was enough to make her knock over the plastic cup.

When Ray Farrar had phoned, Kevin Lomax had said that he was available for a chat for the next hour, before he had to go to catch a train to London. He had an open, friendly face and an untidy mop of black hair. He lived in a small flat on the second floor of what had originally been a very large house built near the end of the Victorian era, and which had since been converted into half a dozen self-contained flats.

He politely offered them coffee, while apologising for it having to be black, which they declined, then invited them to share an old settee which went down considerably under their weight.

Ray Farrar tried to make the visit look a routine one. This, he felt, would put the young man at ease. He had also discovered through the years that a series of questions that appeared generalist and not specific often produced better results than a more intense approach.

"We'd be grateful if you could tell us anything you know about Valerie Salter, Mr Lomax, or how we could get in touch with her. Obviously, we don't wish to pry into people's private lives, but we are trying to speak to as many people as possible who knew both Michael Springer and Dr Delia Bumstead."

He young man said how shocked he'd been on hearing of Delia Bumstead's murder, and it was also obvious that his sadness at Michael Springer's death was tinged with guilt over their falling out. At a few gentle and seemingly casual questions from Mark Newport, he stated that he and Michael Springer had fallen out over Michael's treatment of Valerie Salter, repeating virtually everything that he had said to Frances McAteer. Both policemen also got the impression that what had made matters worse in Kevin Lomax's eyes was that he had had more than a passing interest in Valerie Salter himself.

After a while it was obvious, from the way in which Kevin Lomax started checking his watch, that he was thinking about his train to London. Ray Farrar knew it was time to bring the interview to an end. He got up somewhat laboriously from the creaking settee, followed by his colleague, then asked one more question.

"If you do find out how we can contact Miss Salter, we'd be most grateful, Mr Lomax." He suddenly stopped as he walked towards the door. "Oh, by the way, Mr Lomax, you don't know by any chance where Miss Salter comes from, do you? Is she from this area?"

"Oh, no. She's from Cumbria."

The two policemen tried not to look at each other. "Cumbria?"

"Yes, I remember her saying she was born up in the Lake District somewhere."

"And how old is she, Mr Lomax?"

He laughed. "Twenty-three. I know because our birthdays are only two days apart."

"OK, anyway, we'd better not detain you any further. You've got that train to catch. Thank you very much, Mr Lomax."

"Yes, that's right, Alan," said Ray Farrar, reading his colleague's thoughts, as they walked down the staircase towards the front door. "She's twenty-three…"

"And Delia Bumstead supposedly had her year out from her degree twenty-three years ago, to go around the world…"

"Exactly. Lets start phoning every maternity hospital in Cumbria. They're bound to have records going back twenty-three years…"

"It's OK, Alf, leave the rubbish in the waste paper bin, I'll see to it myself later."

"Are you sure, Dr O'Reilly? I can do it now, if you want me to."

"No, don't worry about it, Alf. You've got enough to do. I know the cleaners and porters are short-staffed."

"It's just that, well, you know…" The man gave an awkward smile. "It's just that some staff can be a bit, er, particular, like…"

Mick grinned. "Bloody awkward and hard to please, always wanting to throw their weight around, you mean, Alf? Don't worry, Paul and I know exactly what you mean – and who you mean, too, I bet, in some cases."

The man visibly relaxed. "Er, there's one thing I've never really understood, actually, Dr O'Reilly."

"What's that, Alf?"

"Well, you know that you're a Senior Lecturer…"

"Yes. Go on."

"Well, is a Principal Lecturer more important, like, than a Senior Lecturer? You know, do they earn more money, like?"

"That's right, Alf."

"Oh, I thought so." The man looked puzzled, and obviously wanted to ask more.

"They teach less hours, too."

"Oh? But if they're called Principal Lecturers, I'd have thought that teaching was what they were best at, what they'd been promoted for…. You know what I mean, like… I'd have thought that if they're Principal Lecturers then they'd principally lecture."

"No, Alf, they principally administrate. An awful cynic, which of course I'm not, would say they principally push paper." He winked. "Or even principally go around arse-licking to have got there in the first place."

The man laughed nervously. "And how long does it take, like, to get promoted?"

"Oh, that depends, Alf. I mean, there's one woman I know of, at a College in London, who went from Lecturer, to Senior Lecturer, to Principal Lecturer, to Head of Department, to Assistant Director within only seven years."

"Ooh, so she moved up really vertically…"

"Well, in her case, horizontally…"

Paul Richardson looked up from marking a script and grinned. He could see that the cleaner had another question to ask.

"Er, you're a doctor, aren't you, Dr O'Reilly? That's your title, like…"

"That's right, Alf."

"Does that mean that you've got a higher qualification than someone called mister?"

"Well, I hate to think of myself in those terms… I supposed I was interested in a particular subject."

"Mmm…"

"Go on, Alf."

"Let me work this out… So Principal Lecturers don't principally lecture… And some of them earn more than you while not being as qualified…"

"That's right, Alf."

"Oh, I see…"

"Then you're a better man than me, Alf."

"How the bloody hell have I let that happen?"

"What's that, sir?" Mark Newport waited until his superior fastened his seat-belt.

"My mobile, I had it switched off…." He stared at the phone for a few seconds. "Oh, God, I don't believe it."

"What is it, sir?"

"A suspicious death, Mark."

"What? Where?"

"In Parkdale St Timothy."

"Not too far from here. Who is it, sir?"

"A nurse at Freelands, you know, the small private hospital."

"How did she die?"

"Run over by a car. More than once, apparently. The body was found in woods in the hospital grounds."

"So it was no accident, then…."

"It would seem not. Hold on a second." He rapidly went through the menu on his mobile, then pressed. "Hello, Gillian, Ray Farrar here. Got any details, then?… Really? I see… And Bill says two to three hours ago, right. That would put it at between eleven and twelve… OK, Gillian, see you back at the College in about a quarter of an hour."

Ray Farrar sighed and stretched back in his seat. "A young woman called Samantha Golightly, Mark. Twenty-seven years of age, divorced. Nurse, worked in the abortion clinic."

"Nothing to do with the College, then, sir," said Mark Newport with a wry smile. "I mean, she isn't a former student, or anything…"

Ray Farrar grunted. "You never know, it might be worth following up. Gillian and Alan are putting details together now. God, a village like Parkdale St Timothy, eh? Who'd have thought it?"

"Not exactly the sort of place you'd associate with a murder, sir."

"No, exactly. Alan's got relatives there. He once said it's one of those places where people's idea of going wild would be to have an *After Eight* mint at seven fifty-five."

Five minutes later, Mark brought the car to a halt outside the main building of the College. He and the inspector got out and dashed from a sudden downpour to find Gillian Taylor and Alan Henry waiting for them in the porch.

"Any further details?"

Gillian Taylor glanced at her notebook as they all walked to the room they were using as an office. "Nothing much as yet, sir. The victim has no link with this place, we've just checked in the files, under both her married name and her former name."

Ray Farrar smiled grimly. "OK, I was wondering the same thing, Gillian. Anything else we know about her?"

"Only that she's divorced, no children. Got divorced six years ago, must have married young. And her former husband lives in Belfast, where he's re-married. He's an accountant. He's been in the firm's office since about half eight this morning."

"So he's out of the frame, then…"

"Bill Foster said he's doing a more detailed check, and will contact you as soon as he's finished."

At that moment there was a knock on the door. Alan Henry got up and opened it.

"Oh, good afternoon, Mr Bumstead."

Ray Farrar immediately got out of his chair. "Mr Bumstead..." He indicated a chair to the side of the desk. He noticed that the man's face had lost its inscrutable, impassive stare. "What can we do for you?" He knew, of course, that it could well be a case of what the man could do for them...

"I have been going through some of my wife's things, Mr Farrar..."

The inspector nodded slowly. "It must be very difficult for you..."

The man went on, as though the inspector hadn't spoken. "And I have found some interesting items."

Ray Farrar tried to appear calm. "What interesting items, Mr Bumstead?"

Without saying anything else, he opened his briefcase, took out an envelope and handed it to the inspector. The envelope contained photographs. Ray Farrar looked at each of them, counting fourteen in all. A young woman appeared in all of them, either on her own or with others, and it was obvious from the background that the photographs had been taken on the college campus. It was obvious, too, from the young woman's change of clothing, her hair style and the surrounding area, that they had been taken at different times of the year, possibly over a lengthy period.

"Where did you find these, Mr Bumstead?"

"In a drawer in my wife's bedroom."

In *my wife's* bedroom... "I see." He held up the photographs. "And can you tell me who the young woman is?"

"I have no idea, Mr Farrar. No idea at all."

"OK. If you don't mind, we'd like to keep the photographs for a while."

The man made a vague hand movement and pulled a face, as though implying that the police could do with them whatever they wished.

"If you come across anything else that you feel may be of interest, Mr Bumstead, we'd be grateful if you'd let us know. Thank you for bringing these."

The man got up from his chair, making an old fashioned, yet somehow extremely polite small bow to Gillian Taylor, then left the room without saying another word.

Ray Farrar let his colleagues look at the photos, then he took three of them and strode purposefully towards the door. "Let's see if anyone recognises her." Seconds later, his heels resounded down the corridor in the direction of the office.

"Any bets on it being a certain former student?" said Mark Newport.

A minute or so later, Ray Farrar returned. He held the photographs in the air, a knowing smile on his face.

"I've just asked the secretary and Mick O'Reilly who it is," he said. "They both said Valerie Salter."

"So she was Delia Bumstead's child... Delia Bumstead had had her that year in Cumbria, when she'd taken a year out..." Gillian Taylor shook her head sadly as she looked at one of the photographs. "She must have gone through agony, seeing her own daughter every day, being unable to tell her..."

"Restricting herself to take photos of her without the girl realising it," added Alan Henry. "A lot of them have been taken from inside, look. You can even see window frames on some of them... God, the poor woman."

"So when Jean-Luc Lafarge saw her crying in town, it must have been when she'd just found out who Valerie Salter was," said Mark Newport.

"And when she refused to teach that group, it must have been because the girl was one of the students in it..." Gillian Taylor handed the photograph back to the inspector. "I wonder if Barry Bumstead knows who she is, or certainly has an inkling..."

She slowly went across to the water cooler, her legs like lead. Another drink of water, she just had to have another drink of water. Her mouth was parched, it hurt her to swallow. It took a few seconds before she realised that a student, a pleasant and polite young man in the first year, was asking her if it was not too late for him to change his mind about one of the second-year options that he had chosen. She nodded, which he took as meaning that it was too late, then she quickly reassured him, somehow stammering a reply, then locked the door once she was alone in the office. She needed to be alone, to collect her thoughts...

She filled her glass with the water, spilling some on the floor, then returned unsteadily to her desk. She sat down, her unfocused eyes staring into nothingness as she thought of the awful implications of that local news flash...

But it couldn't have been him who did it, she thought... *He's been here all morning, he was at that meeting that Cuthbert Bent had chaired, he was there the whole time. He didn't leave the room, and he'd been in quite early for him, at about half eight, twenty to nine... Unless he'd done it before then, very early on, and come into work... No, the news flash somehow implied that it had occurred only a few hours ago...*

She gulped down some water and ran her hand through her hair. *Unless it really was an accident, some hit and run driver, perhaps, someone who'd hit her and then panicked...* More water. *Don't take any notice of the knock on the door, it'll only be some student who can find out what they want to know by looking at some notice board... Yes, it'll just be coincidence that it's her who's been killed... He wouldn't have got the note I'd pushed under his office door until half eight, a quarter to nine, so he wouldn't have been able to get to Parkdale St Timothy, kill her, and then get back here... No, it would have been impossible. He'd been talking to Harold Cassidy at about a quarter to ten, then Dominic Carruthers was in his office for a while, as well... No, it couldn't have been him, it was coincidence, it just had to be...* Just one more glass of water and a parecetamol...

Chapter 13

"There's no way we can allow her to pass, Harold. She just hasn't got the marks. And she doesn't deserve to pass, either. She's failed in practically every area."

The Head of Department gave a tight smile and pushed his glasses up the bridge of his nose. "No, Mick, you're wrong."

Mick O'Reilly stared at the rows of marks on the sheet of paper that he had in his hand, then stared at Harold Cassidy. "Harold, excuse me, but the pass mark is forty per cent. Right?"

"Well, when one says forty per cent-"

"Harold, is the pass mark forty per cent or isn't it forty per cent?"

The Head of Department made a steeple with his fingers. "The underlying approach has to be one of relativity and not absolutism, Mick."

"What in God's name are you talking about, Harold?"

"One has to look at a student's marks in relative terms, not absolute terms..."

"You mean that a student's marks can mean whatever we want them to mean if it suits us?"

"*Interpret,* Mick, not *mean.* I'm saying that there are times when we can interpret a student's mark in certain circumstances."

"Yes – if a student has been ill, or has some awful problem to do with home. I'm the first to help any student like that. But not someone who's a genius at playing the system."

"Mick, where are you coming from?"

"Birkenhead, Harold," he said, exaggerating the scouse accent.

"Mick, this is no laughing matter."

"So there's something we agree on, then," said Mick drily.

"May I cut in here?" said Eric Fisher in a quiet but authoritative voice, his face set in a charming smile.

"Yes, we would, as always, value your contribution and input, Eric," said Harold Cassidy. "You can always see these things so clearly and express them so precisely."

From the corner of his eye Mick O'Reilly could see Paul Richardson silently shake his head in disbelief as he sat at his desk in the corner of the room, marking essays.

As soon as he'd received the joint memo from Harold Cassidy and Eric Fisher bearing the title "Student marks" and requesting a meeting in his office, Mick feared that there was going to be a problem. And his fears were being proved right.

"Mick," said Eric Fisher, his mouth still set in the same smile, "of course I appreciate your concerns. Standards are standards. And nobody believes that more passionately than I. However, when a student fails to obtain the required pass mark of forty per cent, we look at his or her case most carefully, to see if, given any circumstances that may exist, a borderline pass is a possibility."

"I couldn't agree more, Eric," said Mick. "But we aren't talking about a student who has failed narrowly, with an overall average of thirty-eight per cent, say. We're talking about a student who has managed no more than thirty per cent and who failed to attend more than half the lectures."

"But we may have to consider mitigating circumstances…"

"The only circumstance that we can consider, Harold, is that Rachel Foxwood is a born sciver. She's swung the lead here for the past two years. Ask any of the staff. She should have been kicked out last year, at the end of her first year, but wasn't. God knows how or why – probably because of bums on seats."

"Well, no, I wouldn't say she was a sciver, Mick," said Eric Fisher, shaking his head sadly.

Mick looked at him. "She's a sciver, Eric." *Just like you bloody well are,* he thought bitterly. *It takes one to know one. She's just like you – street wise, articulate, a born charmer…*

"But there's a letter here from her parents, Mick, saying that she's been under a lot of stress lately. She's been seeing the doctor for depression ever since she crashed the Aston Martin that they had given her for a birthday present."

Paul was thankful that Mick then laughed out loud, as it drowned his own snigger.

"My God! The world some people must live in! She's heart-broken over crashing her Aston Martin, eh? No wonder she's the type of person she is, if she has a pair of pillocks for parents!"

"Mick, that sounds quite unprofessional," said the Assistant Head of

Department.

Mick looked at him for a few seconds. *Sciving off to play squash and to visit the betting office is bloody unprofessional, you hypocritical bastard...*

"I'm merely stating facts. I am not being the slightest bit unprofessional."

"No matter what the cause, the young woman has been under stress, Mick. Haven't you experienced stress?"

He laughed, mostly to himself. "Me, experience stress, Eric? Let me tell you something. When I was a student, I buried my mother nine weeks before my first Finals paper."

"Yes, well-"

"And in those days, there was no such bloody thing as pleading this or that, or knowing your rights. You just got on with it. There was no queue of people holding my hand or wiping my arse, telling me that there must be hundreds of other problems that I could think about."

"Times have changed, Mick," said Eric Fisher soothingly.

"To the extent that thirty per cent is deemed acceptable for a student to proceed to her final year?"

"Mick, you always support the students, you're well known for encouraging them to get the best out of themselves..."

"Yes, I like to think that, Harold. But I won't lift a finger to help an out and out sciver. Especially when she's mouthy and knows everything about her rights and bugger all about her responsibilities."

Just then, there was an urgent knock on the door. Paul left his marking to open it.

"Oh, hello, Jean-Luc, is it me you want to speak to? It's just that Mick's busy at the moment..." He pointed beyond the door to where Mick was standing with his two visitors.

"Ah, the very men I want to see! You say there is a problem with Rachel Foxwood's marks." He tapped the memo he had been sent. "There has always been a problem with her marks – because they are always awful! She's as lazy as a newt!"

"Mick, Jean-Luc," said Eric Fisher, the smile now beginning to fade. "There are some facts that you should know. Isn't that right, Harold?"

"Oh, yes, yes. Some extremely important facts. Fire away, Eric."

"Rachel's parents, her father especially, can be very persuasive and demanding…"

Mick threw his head back and laughed. "Persuasive and demanding! You mean articulate and pushy. Used to getting their own way with people. The shut-up-and-listen-to-me brigade!"

"Mick." The smile had now disappeared. "Her father's leader of the local Council. He's tipped to become an MP…"

"Oh, so he's in politics, then, is he?" said Mick. "A self important little gobshite on an ego trip, you mean? Oh, well, we must back down to him, then, mustn't we?"

"And her boyfriend is Nigel Jevons, almost certainly the next Student Union President," added Harold Cassidy, his hands joined and shoulders hunched, looking as though he was playing the part of a Victorian undertaker.

"And? So what? Are you saying that we should start kow-towing to mouthy students as well as mouthy parents?"

"Hah!" said the Belgian. "Mon dieu! And this is England, where everything is supposed to be fair and above the board, where there is no skulldigging."

"Duggery, Jean-Luc," said Harold Cassidy.

"Buggery? What do you mean?" shouted the Belgian, having misheard him because of Paul's bout of simulated coughing.

"And how about the other students?" said Mick. "The vast majority of students here are decent, hardworking young men and women who attend lectures, do the assignments that are set. Are we being fair to them?"

"The fact is-"

"And how about a student who fails to get the required minimum mark, but who doesn't have an articulate and pushy middle-class mummy and daddy? Would we be worrying so much about them?"

"We have to face facts, gentlemen," said Eric Fisher, the smile slowly returning. "There are other realities we have to face, as well, in Rachel Foxwood's case…"

"Other realities? And what are they, these other realities?" Mick's sardonic grin went from one man to the other.

"Rachel Foxwood's uncle – her mother's brother – is Fred Biggs, Mick." Eric Fisher emphasised the name.

"Fred Biggs... Is that the bloke who's made a fortune out of his building company?"

"That's right, Mick. And Fred Biggs has been a most generous benefactor to this College, especially since his niece has been a student here – and he's just been approached for work on the new block." Eric Fisher's eyes met Mick's full on. "And he's also implied that the work could be done at a highly competitive price..."

"... if the College behaves itself with his precious niece!" said Mick. "My God..."

"Hah!" said Jean-Luc Lafarge with a knowing grin. "So this is why she is being treated as a special case!" He pointed to his tie. "The old school net boy!"

"This is nothing to do with any old boy network!" said Eric Fisher, almost shouting.

"Oh yes, it is," the Belgian shouted back. "What do the English say -You scratch my bum, and I'll scratch yours!"

"Well, this case will be discussed in full, at the Examination Board, I can promise you that!"

"You're dead right it will, Eric," said Mick grimly.

"OK, let's get a few things clear in our heads." Ray Farrar spoke in hushed tones, knowing that the corridor was busy with passing students and that anyone could overhear from outside the door. "Delia Bumstead must be Valerie Salter's mother. And Valerie Salter was adopted, which means that Delia Bumstead had given her away, presumably almost immediately after she was born. Then, through a fluke, Valerie comes here as a student."

He waited for his colleagues to nod their agreement.

"Now, Delia Bumstead obviously must have found out who she was, after a while. We may never know how, but that seems to have been the case. From what practically everyone says about Delia Bumstead, she made it her business to find out everything about everyone..."

"But she told Liz Goodwin that she'd lost *two* children, sir..." Mark Newport raised a finger as the answer suddenly came to him. "Of course, she meant Valerie Salter *and* the baby that Valerie Salter was expecting..."

"Exactly, Mark," said Ray Farrar. "I think that's almost certainly what she meant. Well, that's how I see it, anyway. Agreed?"

"It certainly fits, sir," said Alan Henry.

"And don't forget that Barry Bumstead told us that throughout their marriage she was unable to have children. Or *more* children, as it turned out. So I assume that when she came across Valerie Salter it must have made it even worse for her. There she is, unable to have children…"

"When the one child she did have, she gave away. And then she ends up seeing her practically every day."

"Exactly, Gillian. No wonder she was difficult to work with. Aye, people's lives, eh… You can see people every day, not knowing what private hell they might be going through."

"And then to top it all, Valerie, the one child she has, has an abortion, as Mark's just said."

"Yes. I wonder… It could have been, couldn't it…"

"It could have been what, sir?" Gillian Taylor edged towards her boss.

"The abortion that Valerie Salter had… I wonder if it was in the clinic at Parkdale St Timothy?"

His colleagues stared at him. Gillian Taylor got up from her chair and walked to the window where she started drumming her fingers on the window sill.

"What you're saying, sir," she said as she turned around, "is that this latest murder could also be linked to the College…"

"Well, linked to Valerie Salter in some way, yes…"

"Is it Valerie Salter who's committed all three of these murders?" said Mark Newport, thinking out loud. He started making a list on his fingers. "She kills Michael Springer for getting her pregnant, making her have the abortion and then deserting her; she kills Delia Bumstead for giving her away when she was a baby; and she kills the nurse Samantha Golightly because she maybe helped with the abortion at the clinic…"

"If Mark's theory holds water, then does that mean other people at the clinic could be in danger?" said Alan Henry.

"Mark's theory is an attractive one," said Ray Farrar, "It doesn't leave many loose ends, for a start. But don't forget that Valerie Salter's file's been taken from the office. That would suggest that if Valerie Salter is responsible for some or all of the murders, she isn't acting alone. It would mean that there's also someone else, probably working here, who doesn't want us to find out anything about her. If it *was* Valerie Salter who took the file, surely someone would have seen her. We've just got to find this young woman. There must be some way of finding out where she lives, there must be someone who knows how to get in touch with her…"

"That was Maureen," said Mick, putting the phone down as Paul came into the office. "It seems her mother's all right. But they're keeping her in hospital for the night, just to make sure. She's prone to fainting, apparently, if she's in a place where there isn't much air. Maureen's sister's with her, so Maureen's coming back in later. She's got a seminar with the second years."

"Oh, I'm pleased her mum's OK," said Paul. "It was certainly a shock to poor Maureen. She went as white as a sheet." He sighed and shook his head.

"What's the matter?"

"Well, I still can't get over Lucinda Hobbs-Smithers actually complaining about the meeting being interrupted. The cow."

"I never know whether to hate people like that, or just feel sorry for them." He pointed towards a small cupboard in the corner of the office. "Coffee?"

Paul glanced at his watch. "Yes, go on, Mick. Just half a cup."

"The trouble with people like Lucinda," said Mick as he poured water into two mugs, "is that, because they think they are someone special, other people pussyfoot around them to avoid confrontation and conflict. But then, because *everyone* pussyfoots around them, they end up *being convinced* that they're someone special. And we all do it."

"Yes, Helen used to work with someone like that. And it's an impossible situation to be in. If you tell them to get stuffed, then there's an awful atmosphere, and things are never the same again."

"So, to keep the peace, you say nothing, and then end up suffering in silence. It's amazing, as well, that in that situation everyone else thinks the same as you, but nobody does or says anything about it."

"That's right," said Paul, with another glance at his watch.

"Who have you got next?"

"The third year poetry lot."

"Oh, God, not them. I've seen more life in Bootle cemetery." Mick was about to take another sip of his coffee but put his mug on the table instead. "That reminds me, speaking of conflict... Maureen's just said that when she was nipping back home from the hospital, she saw Eric Fisher and Lucy Wendover having a bit of a ding-dong in a side road just behind the woods."

"Eric Fisher and Lucy Wendover? I wonder what they were arguing about?"

"I don't know. Maureen said that she only noticed them through stopping the car for a moment to check if she had something with her. And there they were, she said, with Lucy Wendover wagging her finger at him."

"I didn't know they knew each other that well. I wonder what they were doing together..." Paul looked at him from over the rim of his mug. "Something going on between them, perhaps?"

Mick gave a little laugh. "Maybe, though Lucy Wendover must be seven or eight years older than him. I wouldn't put anything past Eric Fisher, I think he's capable of anything. It's strange that they were together, though. If they were arguing about something to do with work..."

"... they'd be doing it here, somewhere on the campus..."

"Exactly," said Mick. "So it could well be about something we're not supposed to know about... That reminds me, after I'd had the argument with Lucy Wendover about her bumping into Liz Farne's car, I noticed that she had a letter addressed to Eric Fisher in the car – addressed to his home, I mean."

"Who had? Lucy Wendover?"

"Yes. I thought it seemed strange at the time. But if there *is* some how's-your-father going on between them, you wouldn't think that Lucy Wendover would have a letter belonging to him in her car, would you, in case her husband saw it..."

"No," said Paul, placing his Lincoln City mug on the table, "I suppose you're right. Anyway, it's time to go and see what the third years have got to tell me about Siegfried Sassoon's war poems."

"It's my bet it wasn't just a hit-and-run accident, Ray. Look at the bruising here, just to the side of the left temple."

145

There were two things about his job that Ray Farrar hated. One was informing relatives or friends of the death of a loved one. And the other was looking at dead bodies, especially the victims of violent or accidental death. So he forced himself to look where Bill Foster was pointing, at the still white face of Samantha Golightly. He noticed that Mark Newport was also trying to avert his eyes as much as possible.

"So what you're saying, Bill, is that she was hit, maybe even killed, before the car ran her over."

The pathologist nodded grimly. "It looks like it, Ray. That injury isn't consistent with the others, which are all on the other side of her body. I know what you're going to ask, and my answer is a cautious yes."

The inspector looked at him intently. "You're saying that she was killed in much the same way that Delia Bumstead was killed...?"

"I'm saying that it's a very strong possibility. And then the person who did it ran her over to make it look like a hit-and-run accident. I can't swear to that, but I'd say it's ninety to ninety-five per cent likely."

"So that the person who did this..."

"I'm only saying that the injury to the side of the head is extremely similar to the injury which caused Delia Bumstead's death, yes, Mark."

"So it's someone with a link to the College..."

"Well, only if Delia Bumstead had some link to Freelands Clinic, Ray," said Bill Foster, peering inquisitively above his glasses as an invitation to him to say more.

"Well, she did have a link to the place, in a rather tenuous way..."

"Go on." The pathologist made a sign to his assistant that the body could now be stored away again.

"Well, we've found out that she had a child when she was a student, and that the same child, just by mere chance, came to the College as a student. She left two years ago."

"You've got me interested, Ray..."

"Well, while she was at College, she had an abortion. And we've just found out that she had the abortion at Freelands."

Bill Foster took his glasses off and cleaned them with a paper tissue. "Well... An interesting coincidence."

"But is it just a coincidence...?"

"Well, that's for you lads – and lasses – to work out, Ray. But I must admit, if I was in your shoes, I would be attracted by the theory of a link..."

"Right... We won't say a word to the press about this, not for the time being, anyway."

"Of course, it *may* be pure coincidence, Ray. There could well be other people connected with the College who've paid similar visits to Freelands. What I'm trying to say is, if it was someone else connected to the College but not directly connected to Delia Bumstead, would you be entertaining the same thoughts?"

"Bloody hell..."

"What have I gone and said, Ray?"

The inspector turned to his colleague, who was staring at him, his mouth slightly open. "You're thinking the same as me, Mark..."

"Liz Goodwin... She said she'd had an abortion..."

"Exactly. And she was Delia Bumstead's one friend on the staff. And Delia was the only person who knew about it..."

"And Liz Goodwin was the only person on the staff who knew that Delia had had a child..."

"Let's find out if Liz Goodwin had the abortion at Freelands." He turned to the bemused pathologist. "You may have opened another can of worms, Bill. Thanks a lot, anyway. Let's know if there's anything else you come across."

"Well, how did Siegfried Sassoon go down, then?"

Paul Richardson dropped his file onto his desk. "Oh, OK, I suppose. Some of them are interested, some of them aren't. Stafford Kingston looked totally bored throughout." He gave a little laugh and shook his head. "What a name, eh? Stafford Kingston."

"Yes," said Mick. "Sounds like a village in Somerset." He mimicked a posh accent. "We came off the M4 at Stafford Kingston, you know."

Their laughter was disturbed by a knock at the door, and Mick opened it.

"What are you grinning at, then?"

"Oh, hi, Maureen. It's OK, Paul and I were just indulging in some schoolboy humour."

"That's most unusual for grown men."

"Ooh, nasty! How's your mother, anyway?"

"Fine, Mick. Just another little scare."

"She's had a do like this before, hasn't she?"

"Oh, yes, two or three. I remember my dad saying that she used to pass out for lack of air even when she was quite young."

"It's still a worry, though, when it happens." He shifted his seating position. "I should see my dad more, I know I should. One of these days something awful's going to happen, and I'll never forgive myself."

"Oh, Mick, it's not as simple as that. You've got your job here, your family, all your responsibilities. You can't be going to Birkenhead every week, or every other week." She held up a hand. "I know it's easy for me to talk, my mum lives very near, and I suppose I've never strayed" – she held up her fingers in the form of inverted commas – "all that far from the area."

"There are people in the family, you know, aunts and uncles, who feel I should be there more, as well."

"Oh, yes. Family know-alls with plenty to say. And that sort of thing makes it worse, makes you feel even more guilty." She punched him playfully. "A good Catholic lad, you see, despite all your protestations to the contrary!"

"He's a worrier deep down, you know," said Paul

"Of course he is, Paul! He was brought up as a Catholic." She pointed to herself. "Of course he's a worrier. From one who knows."

"Hah! I can't think when I was last in church…"

"Same here, Mick. But, as they say, once a Catholic, etcetera, etcetera!" She suddenly stopped smiling. "By the way, speaking, indirectly, of guilt…"

"What?"

"Well, a complete lack of guilt, in this case – Eric Fisher."

"What about him?"

"Well, you know I said I saw him with Lucy Wendover?"

"Oh, yes. You said you saw them before, having a bit of a go at each other. I wonder what that was about?"

"Well, it was her who was having a go at him, to tell the truth. She was actually wagging her finger at him! I couldn't believe it! Can you imagine anyone getting away with wagging their finger at Eric Fisher?"

"Is there something going on between them, do you think, then?"

"I don't know. They're well suited to each other, if there is something going on. I think she's as cold as he is. Whenever I've had any dealings with her, I've always had the impression of someone who's totally self possessed, someone not all that interested in people. She's married, though, isn't she?"

"Yes, her husband's the Head of Parkdale High. If there *is* something going on between them, I wonder if he knows about it? Maybe he does, and just turns a blind eye to it."

"That's most helpful. Thank you very much indeed."

"Well, sir?"

Ray Farrar nodded at Gillian Taylor and then to his other two colleagues. "Yes, Freelands confirms that Liz Goodwin had the abortion there. And," he said, raising a forefinger, "Samantha Golightly was working there then, as well. She'd just started, in fact."

"So we've got to see Liz Goodwin again, sir?"

"Yes, I think so, Mark. It's going to be an awkward one, whether she's involved with Samantha Golightly's death or not. Remember how she was when we interviewed her? God, if we've got to go over details of the abortion with her, I dread to think what she'll be like."

Gillian Taylor studied three sheets of paper that she had stapled together, each sheet bearing the time-table for each student year. "She's teaching at the moment, sir." She looked at her watch. "For another twenty minutes. Then she's not due to teach for another hour."

"Fine, we'll see her then."

"If she's nothing to hide, sir, then it possibly makes our job that little bit easier," said Mark Newport. "What I mean is, the spotlight would then fall more definitely on the link between Delia Bumstead and Valerie Salter."

The inspector pointed to the staff files that were piled on the desk in front of him. "I've gone through these. There's nothing that suggests any link with Delia

Bumstead, the Lake District, or whatever. I thought it wouldn't be that simple."

They sat in silence for a few seconds, the only noise being the outer branches of a clump of trees which, in the wind, scratched against the window as though trying to eavesdrop on the conversation. Then Ray Farrar's mobile rang.

"Ray Farrar... Yes, did you come up with anything?... What? Are you sure?... How many, exactly?... Very interesting, good work... If there's anything else, let me know."

He put the phone away and stared at all his colleagues, his eyes on fire.

"Well, you're going to find this most interesting..."

Chapter 14

"Hello, Rosemary – are you OK?"

She gave a little jump as she realised how close Veronica Makepeace's face was to hers. She swallowed and ran her hand through her hair as she could feel her face going red.

"Oh, sorry, Veronica…"

"It's all right, Rosemary, don't worry. You looked miles away. All this business about Delia is getting to us all, I know." She suddenly dropped her voice. "And have you heard the local news? Someone's been run over and killed out at the Freelands Clinic. A hit-and-run thing, so they say."

She swallowed again. "Er, yes, yes… I heard something about it on the news. Awful. Yes."

"Are you sure you're all right, Rosemary? Can I get you a drink or something?" The woman's concerned eyes looked down at her from the other side of her desk.

"I'm fine, thanks, Veronica. I suppose you're right, it's probably delayed shock over Delia. I still can't believe it."

"Well, I think none of us can. Mind you," she added, after looking behind her to ensure that no-one was there, "some people are just carrying on as normal. You'd think nothing had happened, looking at some people."

"I hate the place."

"Pardon, Rosemary?"

"I said I hate the place. I hate the job." She banged her desk. "I hate some of the people in it. I hate the place."

Veronica Makepeace hurried around the side of the desk to comfort the secretary the second she saw her mouth tremble. She drew up a chair next to hers and put her arm around her shoulder. A few moments later, Harriet Bond walked into the office.

"Good God! You're at it again! The second my back's turned!"

"Harriet, don't be silly! I'm just trying to comfort Rosemary."

The woman threw her head back and cackled. "Hah! I can see that! You're very good at comforting other women, aren't you? That's the second time I've caught you!"

"Harriet, now that's just being stupid. There's no need-"

"I've had enough! I can't take any more excuses!"

Harriet Bond turned around and swept out of the office, banging her hip against a cupboard near the door, uttering a mild swear word as she did so.

"Don't take any notice of her, Rosemary, love. You know what she's like. Are you sure you don't want me to get you anything?"

She delicately blew her nose into a paper handkerchief that Veronica Makepeace had plucked out of a box for her. "No, thanks, Veronica. I'm all right, honestly. Thank you, anyway."

"I've got to go and teach, Rosemary. But I'm free in an hour's time, if you need me."

"Thanks, Veronica. I'll be OK, don't worry." She gave a tight, forced smile. "I'll make myself a coffee. Thanks for your concern."

She watched Veronica Makepeace leave the office, and got up to put the kettle on. She was about to pour water onto the spoonful of coffee when the phone rang. It was her daughter, Michelle, asking her if she could remind her father about the sheet music he had promised to obtain for her during his business trip to London, where he was staying overnight.

She replaced the receiver, took out her mobile, and dialled her husband's mobile number. She sighed with exasperation when it was obvious that he had switched it off. She knew the number of the hotel where he was staying, so she phoned there instead.

"The Formby." Despite the attempt at disguising it, the voice had a slight cockney accent.

"Can I leave a message for Mr Colin Hepworth, please?"

"Yes, certainly. Do you have his room number?"

"I don't, I'm afraid."

"It's OK. Oh, you've just missed him, actually, he's just gone out."

That's strange, she thought, *he said he would be at a meeting all afternoon.* "Just gone out? Are you sure?"

"Yes, they went out just a few minutes ago."

"They?"

"Yes, he and his wife. What's the message you'd like me to pass on to him?"

152

She stared into space, everything becoming a blur. All she was aware of was the phone clattering onto the desk.

"Well, the assignment is quite acceptable, Anne." Veronica Makepeace nodded her head sagely before handing it to the student.

Anne Dickinson took it and looked at the mark. "Oh, good, fifty-five per cent. I wasn't expecting that."

The woman looked at her from over her glasses. "Really? Is that because you didn't spend enough time on it?"

Anne's face went red. "Oh, er, no."

"Or are you happy with fifty-five because you're easily pleased with that sort of mark?"

"No, of course not." She could feel her face going even redder as she picked a hair off her jeans. "I don't think it's right that students should question marks all the time, that's all. Some people seem to be professional moaners."

The woman laughed. "Oh, I don't mind that, Anne. I'm all for people standing up for themselves and not taking things lying down. Things can be exciting if you refuse to accept life's little diktats."

"It's just that Social Policy isn't one of my strong points, that's all. I have trouble putting my point across sometimes, and find that I end up contradicting myself."

The woman played with a pencil, its exquisitely sharp point looking fragile. "I see. One of your problems, Anne..." – she sighed and shook her head in a world-weary way – "is that you can be somewhat conservative in your thinking, especially with regard to the family unit."

"I'm sorry, I don't quite understand..."

"Well, in the essay you constantly argue as though a two-parent family is the norm for society..."

Anne pulled a face and hunched up her shoulders. "Well, I think it is, or think it should be..."

"Why do you think that, Anne?"

She played with a thin bracelet that decorated her right wrist. "I suppose it's because it's what my parents have taught me…"

Veronica Makepeace stopped playing with the pencil and smiled. "Oh, if only you knew how conventional that sounds, Anne! We don't necessarily have to accept without thinking what we have been told by our parents, you know. That's what personal development and awareness is all about…"

"Oh, yes, I know that…" She felt uncomfortable, somehow, and just wanted the conversation to either come to an end or to change course. The lecturer's next question seemed to imply that her second wish had been granted.

"Anyway, how are you feeling, Anne? What you saw must have been an awful shock for you."

She swallowed, partly relieved at the change of tack. "Yes, I keep thinking about it. I can't get it out of my mind."

"And there's nothing else you can remember about any of it, Anne? I mean, you know, immediately before or after?"

She shook her head, her gaze going from the woman's eyes to the raindrops spattering the window. "No, nothing at all. All I can remember afterwards is being in nurse Richmond's office with some of my friends."

The woman reached across and patted the back of her hand. "Well, if ever you want to talk about anything, Anne, you know where to find me…"

She smiled awkwardly, feeling her blush coming back. "Oh, er, thank you… Can I go now?"

It was only when the woman burst out laughing that she realised how childlike the question must have sounded.

"Yes, of course – I think that's all I have to say about your assignment, Anne." The stare came from over the glasses again. "But don't belittle yourself. You can do well, with the right guidance. We'll have another chat sometime, about which options you'd like to do next year. And don't forget – if anything suddenly comes to mind to do with your horrible experience, don't hesitate to come and tell me about it."

Anne left the room and went out of the building, thankful to be breathing fresh air, despite the rain hitting her face and soaking her hair.

To her right, she could see Geraldine Murphy and Liz Farne going into the student union building. She decided to follow them, thinking that a coffee and a good chinwag would be a welcome distraction from the strange encounter she had just had with Veronica Makepeace. Besides, she knew Liz Farne was looking for some part-time work, so she could ask Liz if she wanted her to mention her name at the café where she worked.

She shaped her body as she was about to run against the rain, then suddenly stopped as a thought hit her.

Liz Farne...Good grief, yes, that's right...No, surely not... She looked back towards Veronica Makepeace's office, breathing heavily. *But I'm not going to mention it to you,* she thought.

"I do have a lot of things to see to..." She went to say more, but found that all she could do was swallow as she stared at each of the four police officers.

Ray Farrar had placed five chairs in a circle so as to make the situation appear as non-adversarial as possible. But even this didn't prevent the woman from trembling, her face drained and white as she tugged nervously at her skirt.

"Mrs Hepworth, as I'm no doubt you're aware, there has been a suspicious death at Freelands Clinic, at Parkdale St Timothy. The victim is a nurse called Samantha Golightly. Do you know her?"

She swallowed again and shook her head, her hands clasped together. "No," she managed to force out.

"Are you sure?"

"Yes, I'm sure."

"Then how do you account for the fact that, on her itemised phone bill, your home number appears no fewer than five times in the past fortnight alone?"

She could feel her head spinning. Her eyes were suddenly unfocused, the voice thick and indistinct. She was suddenly aware of Gillian Taylor kneeling next to her, peering up at her and asking if she wanted some water. She shook her head, slowly and silently, as she tried to piece together her thoughts.

Well, Colin's having an affair, too. That means it doesn't matter so much if he knows about what I've been doing...

She was also horribly amused by the fact that, hurtful though her discovery of her husband's infidelity was, it also helped to liberate her from the nightmare that she had created for herself...

But she was also still in a state of shock at Samantha Golightly's death. What if it hadn't been an accident? But who had done it, if it was murder? *It couldn't have been him, he'd been in the building or just outside it the whole morning. So if Samantha Golightly's death was murder, had he got someone else to do it for him?*

The thought was frightening, for it implied that her own life could possibly be in danger. So she decided that she would tell this policeman why her home number had appeared on Samantha Golightly's itemised phone bill – but limit it to that and nothing else...

"Mrs Hepworth, if you'd please answer the question..."

"She was blackmailing me, inspector." She surprised herself at how calm she suddenly was.

They all looked at her, their faces deadpan.

"I see," said the inspector after a few seconds. "And why was she blackmailing you, Mrs Hepworth?" He could guess why, but knew he had to ask.

"Because I had an abortion there."

"But why did she know that you could be blackmailed because of it?"

"Because she probably guessed that the baby wasn't my husband's." Her lip quivered a little, then she quickly regained her composure, though she was no longer making eye contact.

"I see." Ray Farrar changed his sitting position, though his eyes remained glued on her. "And were you driving the car that ran her over, Mrs Hepworth?"

"No, I wasn't. I had nothing to do with it."

"Were you in the car when it ran her over?"

"No, I wasn't. As I said, I had nothing to do with it. I don't know anything about it."

Her responses were calm, measured, to the point, almost embodying her professional secretarial skills. He was convinced that she was telling the truth – or, to be more exact, she was answering these specific questions truthfully.

"But do you know who did it, Mrs Hepworth?"

"No, I don't."

"Have you any idea who could have done it?"

"No, I haven't." She looked him in the eye. "I mightn't have been the only person she was blackmailing, of course."

He returned her gaze and said nothing for a few seconds. It was a possibility that he had entertained himself. Presumably there were other women who had had abortions at the clinic without telling their husbands, and who were therefore potential blackmail victims. But he knew that what had interested him was that this particular blackmail victim had a link with Parkdale College... He was also aware, and Mark Newport had also stated this, that many extra-marital affairs occur through work. So had the father been someone at Parkdale College, he wondered...

"The father of the child, Mrs Hepworth...," he said, his eyes unblinking as they stayed on hers, "does he work here?"

She reddened. "I don't see what relevance that has."

Ah, interesting. So it was someone who works here.

"Mrs Hepworth, we are conducting a murder investigation. Possibly *three* murder investigations – the student Michael Springer, Delia Bumstead and Samantha Golightly. There is a common strand, or link, between them, however tenuous in your own particular case. And that common strand is Parkdale College. So I'll ask you again: is the person who made you pregnant one of your colleagues?"

She thought of her husband again. *He's seeing someone else behind my back – God knows what they get up to. He's going to find out about the abortion – so why shouldn't he find out who the father was?*

"Yes, it was someone who works here."

"May I ask who?"

A sudden gust blowing rain against the window temporarily shattered the silence as they waited for her reply.

"Eric Fisher."

"The Assistant Head of Department?"

"Yes."

"And what was his reaction when you told him you were pregnant?"

"He didn't want to know. He said it could be my husband's. I told him that was impossible, because my husband had a vasectomy eight years ago."

"And what did he say then?"

"He said I was to get rid of it – in his words."

157

"And what was your reaction?"

"More or less the same. I was terrified as to how my husband would react."

"So when did the operation take place?"

"Two months ago. He paid for it."

"Who, Eric Fisher?"

"Yes."

Ray Farrar's mind went back to the interview with Liz Goodwin. *Had Eric Fisher been the father of her baby, too*, he wondered... A check would have to be done to see if Liz Goodwin's phone number figured prominently on Samantha Golightly's list of phone calls...

Gillian Taylor and Alan Henry exchanged a glance, each knowing what the other was thinking: the conversation that they had overheard between Eric Fisher and Dominic Carruthers, where Eric Fisher's ambitions for promotion had been obvious. And those ambitions would receive a severe setback in a College which still had links with the Church... So it was natural that he wanted the woman to have an abortion. And she, presumably, would have wanted to hide the truth from her husband...

"And did Eric Fisher know that you were being blackmailed by Samantha Golightly?"

She was silent for a few seconds. "Yes."

"And what did he say to that?"

"He said that she wasn't to know that he had been the father, and that some solution had to be found."

"And did Samantha Golightly know that he had been the father?"

"No. I never told her, anyway."

"Thank you, Mrs Hepworth. We may want to speak to you again."

"There is one other thing, inspector."

"And what is that?"

"I fear for my own safety."

"Why?"

"Well, this morning, I left Eric Fisher a note, telling him that I just couldn't carry on being blackmailed by that woman, that I was at the end of my tether, and that something had to be done."

"Yes..."